CONTENTS

AND THEN THEY WERE GONE

A DCI PETER MOONE CHRISTMAS NOVELLA

MARK YARWOOD

EXCLUSIVE OFFER

Look out for the link at the end of this book or visit my website at www.markyarwood.co.uk to sign up to my no-spam Monthly Murder Club and receive two FREE and exclusive crime thrillers plus news and previews of forthcoming works.

Never miss out on a release.

No spam. You can unsubscribe at any time.

For my wife, daughter and Mittens

ONE

The snow was coming down fast, coating the Dartmoor landscape, a white blanket thrown over the darkening ground, swallowing the road ahead.

The wipers on Mandy Butler's car screamed, moaning that they were having to work too hard as the snowflakes layered the windscreen. To Moone, who was sitting forward, staring out into the darkness, visibility seemed to be a fading memory. The radio was on but was turned down low, voices muttering away.

The darkness was settling in early and now their headlights beamed ahead but only caught the swirling snow, giving the impression they, and the blizzard, were trapped in a dark tunnel.

'I knew we should've stayed on the A38,' he said, then sighed and sat back, listening to the hum of the heater. There were only a couple of days until Christmas and he hadn't bought a single present yet. He had planned a little late night Christmas shopping but now that had gone out the window.

Butler huffed as her hands gripped the wheel, bent over it, staring into the nothingness beyond the windscreen. 'I'm very sorry if my delivering of presents has inconvenienced you, Moone. I didn't know there was going to be a bloody blizzard, did I?'

He grunted, leaning forward, as if that would help them see through the blur of white. 'Yeah, well, maybe next time you can use the post, Santa.'

She rolled her eyes, the corner of her mouth twitching. 'Well, next time, I'll leave you in Exeter.'

Butler edged the car on a little way. The car crawled along the narrow lane, the snow-laden hedgerows rising on either side, appearing like ghostly shapes. The tyres crunched and slipped over the uneven ground as the wind picked up, driving more snow sideways. The Dartmoor landscape, which was normally vast and haunting to Moone, seemed to close in around them. The moor itself had been swallowed by the storm. Moone decided to turn the radio up a little. 'Let's hear what's happening to the roads.'

'...and police are warning motorists to be cautious tonight as snow continues to fall heavily across large parts of Devon. Authorities are advising against travel across the moors unless absolutely necessary.'

Moone shifted in his seat, muttering, 'Well, that's us told.'

Butler smirked, keeping her eyes on the ghostly road ahead.

The presenter's tone changed, a hint of tension tightening his words as he said, 'In other news, police have confirmed that a prisoner has escaped from custody earlier this evening while being transported from Channings Wood Prison. The man, thirty-nine-year-old Raymond Keel, was serving a life sentence for multiple violent offences, including armed robbery and several brutal murders. Officers have launched a large-scale search across the moor, where he was last seen, although the bad weather has forced the search…'

A hiss of interference filled the car before the voice broke through again.

'…Members of the public are advised not to approach Keel under any circumstances. He is considered dangerous and may be seeking shelter from the worsening weather. Anyone who sees anything suspicious is urged to contact the police immediately.'

The radio crackled with static once more, the signal fading in and out, mixing with the howl of the wind.

Moone sighed as he shook his head. 'Great. A blizzard and a violent convict on the loose. Perfect night for a drive through Dartmoor.'

Butler shot him a sideways look. 'You think he's out here? If he's got any sense, he's found somewhere warm to lie low. Or he's already frozen to death.'

'As long as he keeps out of our way.' Moone turned to his window and stared out, his breath fogging the glass. He thought he saw something in the distance, a few hundred yards beyond the narrow lane. Lights.

'Hang on,' he said, tapping the glass. 'Lights.

Looks like a village.'

Butler looked over, squinting as she eased her foot off the accelerator. Through the drifting white glow of falling snow, lights flickered in the distance.

Moone unbuckled his seatbelt. 'Pull over. I'll take a look.'

'Moone, hang on,' she started to say, but he already had the door open, battling against the wind and snow. The cold bit into him, the driving snow stinging his skin as he hunched his shoulders and pulled his coat tighter around him. He trudged forward, his shoes crunching into the ever-deepening snow. He shielded his eyes as he squinted, looking over the white hedgerows and into the distance. There was a cluster of warm lights about four hundred yards away. It looked very much like a small village to Moone. He could make out a small gathering of buildings, a scattering of cottages huddled together around an old stone church, its spire ghostly under the white haze. At the centre of it all stood a large country pub, all wood beams and windows where warm light glowed out to him. The place looked as if it had been standing since the Normans had invaded. Smoke was rising from a chimney and up into the white and black sky.

There was something about the scene, a strange silence, apart from the moaning of the wind and the rumble of the car's engine. There was little movement, just the empty white ground that surrounded the village. It looked almost as if the village was the last outpost on earth, set on an endless white desert.

Moone trudged back to the car, brushing his coat off before climbing inside. 'Head for the lights. There's a pub and it looks open.'

Butler glanced at him. 'A pub? Out here? You sure you're not seeing things?'

Moone took out his phone, ready to check where they were exactly. No signal. 'Well, we either head for that pub or we freeze to death waiting for your Christmas spirit to thaw the road.'

She gave a short huff, then shifted into gear. 'Cheeky sod. Fine. Let's see if they serve coffee… or better still, whisky.'

Butler edged the car forward through the white silence, the tyres slipping as they reached a turning. There was a small sign that read Scurry-on-the-Moor.

Moone turned to Butler and saw her staring out towards the lights, the engine still grumbling away.

'What're we doing?' he asked.

She sighed, then took the car into the village. The pub loomed larger now, a sign swinging on creaking hinges: The Scurry Inn. Butler parked as close as she could and then they made a dash for it, their heads down as the snow bit at their faces.

By the time they reached the heavy oak door, both of them were dusted white, shivering and laughing despite themselves. Butler pulled the door open, and a wave of warmth and golden light met them along with a welcoming scent of ale that reached Moone's nostrils.

The place was quiet, but certainly not empty. A handful of figures were sitting near the fire, most of them turning slowly as the door closed behind Moone and Butler.

The warmth inside The Scurry Inn wrapped around them like a thick blanket, a whole world away from the biting cold outside. Moone rubbed his cold hands as he examined the place. It looked as if it hadn't changed in a hundred years, maybe longer. The air smelled of smoke, hot food and pine from the real but small Christmas tree in the far corner. The ceiling was low, crossed with blackened beams that sagged with age. A real fire roared in the wide hearth, its light flickering gold and amber shapes over the walls. Along the walls were hung crooked rows of old black-and-white photos: farmhands posing beside tractors, huntsmen on horseback, and there was one of the pub itself, snow piled high outside just as it was tonight.

A whippet stirred near the fire, lifting its narrow head to watch Moone and Butler before it got bored and closed its eyes again. It was a grey-faced and wiry dog that had probably seen many winters. Its owner was a man in his seventies with a weathered face and hands covered in liver spots. He nodded to them but said nothing. He wore a thick cardigan with leather patches on the elbows as he sat nursing half a pint.

'Come on, get comfy,' a voice said from across the room. A full-figured woman was standing behind the bar. She was in her late forties, cheeks pink from the heat, her hair pinned up in a messy bun. Her smile seemed to shine bright, lighting up the dim room.

'Evening,' she said, wiping her hands on a towel. 'You two look half frozen. Get yourselves warm by the fire.'

'This doesn't seem too bad,' Butler whispered to Moone as they stepped towards the bar.

Moone nodded, still looking round the place. A young couple were sitting to the right of the fire. They seemed a complete contrast to each other; the lad, dark-haired, brooding, and silent, wore a bright yellow hoodie that looked almost fluorescent in the firelight. His girlfriend had hay-coloured hair that fell loose over her shoulders. When she turned and smiled at Moone and Butler, there seemed to be a genuine warmth in her eyes and maybe even a little apology for her boyfriend's sullenness. The young lad didn't return the gesture; he just stared at the table, fingers tapping a slow rhythm against his pint glass.

'I'm Hannah,' the young girl said. 'This is Tom.'

'Pete,' Moone said and was about to introduce Butler. As he wondered what to announce her as, he caught her glare and decided to say, 'This is… Butler.'

Butler huffed as she stood at the bar, smiled and brushed the snow from her coat. 'We thought we were going to be stuck out here. I'm glad you're open.'

The landlady laughed softly. 'Oh, we're always open. Storm or no storm. I'm Maggie. Pint? Coffee, tea? Mulled wine?'

'Coffee,' Moone said, automatically. 'Black.'

'Give him a whisky to go with it,' Butler said and nudged Moone.

He nodded. 'And a whisky, thanks.'

Maggie winked. 'Good man. Make yourselves comfortable.'

As Butler shrugged off her coat, a door creaked open behind them. Moone turned to see a man emerging from a dark and narrow corridor that seemed to lead to the toilets. He was a stocky figure in his forties wearing a green coat, flat cap, and worn jeans tucked into muddy boots. He paused when he saw them, his gaze lingering a little too long. It wasn't exactly a hostile look, Moone decided but there was a definite expression of caution.

He gave a small nod, then moved to a table in the far corner, where he picked up a half-drunk pint and kept them in sight.

Moone caught the look. Years of policing had taught him to notice when he was being watched. There was something in the air, he sensed, despite the warmth and friendliness of the landlady. But he said nothing to Butler as he moved closer to the fire, letting the warmth seep into his bones. The whippet gave a small huff and curled back into sleep.

The door opened again and a gust of icy air rushed in, scattering snowflakes across the wooden floor.

It was a woman who stepped through the low doorway. She was in her mid-thirties, dark hair in a loose bob coming from beneath a woollen hat, snow glittering on her red raincoat. She was attractive with sharp, carved features in a pale face. Her cheeks were flushed from the cold, her lips bright red with lipstick. She stamped her boots and shut the door quickly behind her.

'God,' she said, catching her breath. 'It's getting worse out there.'

Maggie leaned on the bar, nodding. 'You're not wrong. Looks like we've got ourselves a proper eve of Christmas Eve blizzard.'

The woman smiled faintly, brushing snow from her shoulders. 'The perfect night to be stuck on Dartmoor,' she said, glancing around the room. Her eyes landed on Moone and Butler.

'More newcomers,' the woman said. 'Welcome to the middle of nowhere. I'm Alma.'

'Pete,' Moone said and took the delicate, pale hand she held out to him. She seemed icy to the touch. 'This is Butler.'

Alma smiled politely to Butler, then looked at Moone again. 'I hope you're not on a winter honeymoon or a Christmas getaway.'

'Oh, we're not,' Moone started to say, and looked at Butler.

'We're colleagues,' Butler said, handing Moone his coffee with a huff.

The woman eyed them both, seeming to nod and smirk before she ordered a gin and tonic.

For a moment, the crackle of the fire was the only sound. Then Maggie poured the whisky and slid it across the bar.

'Looks like you're all here for the night,' she said cheerfully, as if she was glad of the company. 'The roads'll be impassable soon.'

'They already are,' a deep voice said to their left.

Moone looked round and saw they had missed the man sitting in a large, battered leather chair in the corner. He wore a pinstriped suit jacket and had a tie hanging loose around his neck. He was in his early forties, Moone decided, and had thick, reddish-brown hair. His blue eyes were dug deep in his pale, clean-shaven face.

'You can call me John,' he said, lifting a mug of something hot as if to raise a toast.

'Is that your name?' Butler asked, lifting her glass of whisky to her lips. 'Or just what we can call you?'

John raised his shoulders, staring at Butler, no sign of a smile on his face. 'A man's got to keep an air of mystery, hasn't he? If you ask me, people share too much these days. Social media and all that crap... people know everything about you... even your darkest secrets.'

Moone exchanged a look with Butler, half amusement, half unease. He had a feeling the eve of Christmas Eve on Dartmoor was about to get a lot longer than either of them had planned.

TWO

'What's your darkest secret, John?' Alma asked, a smile on her red lips as she sat down at a small table by the door. She eyed him briefly before she turned her attention back to her gin and tonic.

Moone watched the man in the corner as he raised his narrowed eyes at her. 'That would be telling, sweetheart, wouldn't it?'

Alma smirked. 'Before I lost my 4G signal, I read that there's a prisoner on the loose tonight. Escaped from Dartmoor.'

'Everyone's escaped from Dartmoor,' John said. 'They closed it. Because of the radon.'

'She's right,' Butler said. 'He was being transported from Channings Wood.'

The young girl, Hannah, spun around and stared at Butler, her eyes wide. 'Really? Is he dangerous?'

'Extremely.' Alma smiled at her, seeming to revel in the girl's horror and discomfort.

'She's pulling your leg,' Tom said with a grunt.

'I'm not,' Alma said and looked towards Moone and Butler as they both sat at a table at the end of the long bar. 'Ask the police over there.'

Moone's head bobbed up. He stared at the woman and saw she had one eyebrow raised, the corner of her red lips turned up.

'How did I know you two were coppers?' Alma asked as she swirled the ice in her glass. 'It's written all over you.'

'Aren't you clever?' Butler said and drank most of her whisky.

'I seem so sometimes,' Alma said, looking into her drink, losing her smirk. 'Depends what company I'm in.'

Moone had been staring at the sleeping dog and deciding he wanted to turn the subject away from escaped convicts. 'What's your dog called?'

The old man's wrinkled eyes fluttered as he sat up. 'This old boy? This is Rusty. He's going on fourteen years. On his last legs. Sleeps most of the day. But so do I, I suppose.'

'Pete,' Moone said and went over and stroked Rusty.

'George,' the old fella said, smiling at his dog that barely responded to Moone's touch.

'What's he done, this escaped prisoner?'

The question had come from the man in the flat cap and the green coat. His voice was low, a little croaky. His eyes were fixed on Alma.

'He's a murderer,' Butler said. 'But don't anyone start scaring themselves thinking he's out there. He'll be miles away.'

'In this weather?' Alma laughed, and shook her

head.

'It's not him you've got to worry about,' George said, smoothing his trembling hand over Rusty's fur. The dog yawned.

'Who should we be worried about?' Moone said and laughed. He stopped when he saw the look of seriousness in the old man's eyes.

'Two hundred years ago, in this very village,' George said as the rest of the pub grew quiet, 'a man was hanged for murder. Joseph Hood. He was charged with the murder of a young woman. She was found in a barn, cut to pieces. Anyway, they determined it was Hood. He'd been seen talking to the girl. They didn't go in for much detection back then, I guess. So they hanged him, right out there.'

'What a load of rubbish,' Tom said and scoffed. 'Clickbait.'

'He's right,' Maggie said, leaning on the bar. 'Out there in the middle of the village, there's a solid wood post. That's where they hanged him. Thing is, it wasn't him who killed her.'

'It wasn't?' Moone sat up, putting his hands round his mug of coffee.

'Nah,' George said, staring Moone in the eyes. 'No one bothered to check where he'd been around the time she died. Didn't bother with that sort of detail. Turned out he'd been shacked up with the landlady of this very pub.'

Maggie laughed. 'Not me. I'm not that old.'

'Did they get the bleeder who really did it?' Butler asked.

The old man shook his head slowly. 'No such luck. He was long gone by then. Some reckon he took off on a boat from Plymouth and started a new life in Australia.'

'Two hundred years ago?' Moone asked.

George stood up with a groan and dusted himself down. 'Two hundred years ago today. And to make matters worse, right before he was hanged, protesting his innocence, he swore he'd come back one day and get his revenge.'

The pub grew quiet again, only the wind whistling outside, and the crackle of the fire to fill the void until Tom gave a laugh.

'What a load of crap,' he said, zipping up his hoodie.

'Tom!' Hannah snapped at him.

Tom shrugged. 'Well, it is. It's all clickbait. I'm not buying it.'

'Clickbait?' Alma said. 'This is real life, sweetheart. No one's trying to sell you anything.'

The old man moved slowly towards the toilet, stopping only to pat Tom on the back. 'Believe it or not, lad, but I suggest you don't go outside on a night like this.'

Tom shrugged off his hand, so the old man headed through the toilet door. An icy cold breeze cut through the room as the door opened and shut.

It was the turn of the man in the flat cap and boots to get up. He searched his coat and then brought out a pack of cigarettes and slipped one between his lips.

'Time for a smoke,' he said, taking out a lighter, his eyes flickering over everyone in the pub.

'It wouldn't be wise to go out in this,' the landlady said as she wiped the bar top.

'Are you going to let me smoke in here?' Flat cap asked with a grumbling laugh.

'Nope,' Maggie said. 'Maybe it's time to give it up.'

'I'll take my chances,' the man said, shaking his head as he made for the door. He quickly lit his cigarette, then pulled open the door, a whirlwind of snow blowing into the pub as he slipped out into the dark.

Moone caught the waft of cigarette smoke and took in a hungry breath.

'Dream on, Moone,' Butler said, then pushed his whisky towards him. 'Drink up and warm your cockles.'

Then Butler looked towards the landlady as she asked, 'Who's the smoker?'

Maggie wiped her hands on a tea towel and nodded towards the door. 'Mr Warren. He's staying here. He's renting one of our small rooms upstairs. Didn't tell me his first name. Quiet fella, but seems friendly enough.'

John, who had been staring into his mug, turned in his chair. 'It's the quiet ones you've got to watch out for,' he said, his lips curling into something between a smirk and a sneer. 'Maybe he's the escaped murderer.'

The landlady scoffed. 'Don't be daft. He arrived

before that was on the news.'

'Maybe the radio was slow to get the word out,' John said, taking another sip of whatever he was drinking. His blue eyes seemed to gleam in the firelight.

Butler turned her head towards him. 'All right, clever clogs, so when did you get here?'

John tilted his head, thinking it over, then gave a small shrug as he smiled. 'I can't remember exactly, to tell the truth.'

'You got here two hours ago,' Maggie said, without hesitation. 'I pay attention.'

'So you could be the prisoner on the run,' Butler said, folding her arms, glaring at him.

John's eyebrows lifted, full of amusement. 'Do I look like an escaped killer?' He pointed at his chest, then gestured at his clothes. 'This is a very expensive suit.'

Moone leaned back in his chair. 'Maybe you did away with the man who owned the suit and put it on. How do we know?'

John's gaze flicked to him, the humour in his face having evaporated. For a long, uncomfortable moment he just stared, eyes as cold as the snow, unblinking. Then he gave a slow nod.

'Maybe you're right,' he said softly. 'Maybe I could be the killer. Let's hope the lights don't go out. Because if they did, and I was the killer...' He paused, letting the silence stretch on for a moment. '...I'd go for the coppers first.'

No one laughed.

The fire crackled, sending a shower of sparks up the chimney. Alma had been looking towards John, but she turned away, her expression tense. Moone looked over to Hannah as she moved, reaching her arm over the table to take hold of Tom's hand. He pulled it away as he muttered something under his breath.

Moody little sod, Moone thought and hoped Alice's boyfriend didn't behave like that.

'Well, it's got gloomy in here,' Maggie said a little loudly as she forced a laugh. 'I don't think we need any of that talk. Nobody's killing anyone in my pub. Come on, we've got warmth, drink, and plenty of food. Let's enjoy being out of that storm.'

'But if someone does decide to… knock someone off,' Alma said, lifting her drink as her eyes fell on Moone. 'We've got the strong arm of the law ready to solve the mystery, haven't we? Swear you'll protect us, Mr Policeman?'

'Scout's honour.' Moone tried to smile as he met her gaze. There was a subtle, playful smile on her lips. She was certainly very attractive, he decided, but there was something below the surface he sensed, something he didn't think he would like.

'You heard the lady,' Butler said, getting to her feet. 'Let's try and keep it festive. Christmas is in two days. I'll buy a round.'

John raised his mug in mock salute. 'I can be festive if someone else is buying me a drink. And I'll really try not to murder anyone.'

Moone listened to him laughing to himself,

then focused on the wind that was groaning against the old windows, making them rattle a little. The door rattled too, as if someone was trying to get through. Everyone turned towards it, half expecting a newcomer to burst in from the blizzard.

'Just Warren trying to get back in,' Maggie said, then shouted, 'Push the door!'

Rusty lifted his narrow head, ears twitching, and gave a low growl, his eyes fixed on the door. Then he yawned and nestled down again.

Butler leaned closer to Moone as she brought back another couple of drinks for them. Her voice was barely a whisper. 'Tell me you've got that weird feeling too about all this?'

'Yes, I certainly do,' he murmured, staring at the door. 'I feel like we're waiting for something and it's not just Christmas.'

'This is going to be a long night. Promise me Moone that if I'm the first one to get murdered, you'll avenge me.'

He saw her smile a little, so said, 'Scout's honour. But nothing's going to happen.'

She rolled her eyes and took a sip of whisky.

Almost as if to prove him wrong, the lights flickered. Once. Twice.

Then the room plunged into darkness.

For a heartbeat, no one said a thing. The fire continued to roar, the orange and black shadows flickering across the low ceiling and the walls.

From somewhere near the entrance came a sound, a dull thud, then the faint rattle of the latch.

Maggie's voice came again, tight now: 'Warren? That you?'

There came no reply.

Moone stood up, his hand going instinctively into his coat pocket for his phone so he could use its torch. It wasn't there. Had he left it in the car? The wind wailed outside, and over it came another sound: it was the squeak of the pub sign swinging wildly on its hinges.

Butler rose beside Moone. He kept his eyes fixed on the door as she said, 'Maybe he's got lost.'

'Maybe he didn't get very far,' John said behind them in the dark. 'Maybe the Dartmoor hands got him or better still, maybe Hood has come back for his revenge.'

Moone turned to try to find John in the dark. Flickering light from the fire caught John's face. His expression was unreadable, his eyes reflecting the flames.

The lights flickered on again and everyone let out a collective sigh of relief.

'See,' Maggie said with a nervous laugh. 'Just a temporary power cut. Nothing to worry about.'

Then the toilet door creaked open and the old man, George, came edging through. He stopped dead when he must have sensed the room's eyes on him. He looked them all over.

'What's happened?' he said and started walking back to his table.

'Your friend, Joseph Hood, cut the lights,' Alma said with a smirk.

George eyed her as he moved past her table, his expression cold. 'It's nothing to laugh about, young lady. Strange, unexplainable things happen on nights like this.'

'Let's have another drink,' Maggie said, and for a moment Moone thought she was going to suggest a chorus of Roll Out The Barrel.

'Where is he?'

Moone looked up and saw George was standing, facing his table, his body frozen. He got up and moved towards the old man.

'Where's Rusty?' the old man flung himself round, his eyes jumping to everybody in the bar. 'Where is he? Where'd he go?'

'Don't look at me,' John said. 'I hate dogs. Stupid animals.'

'Where is he?!' George demanded.

'Calm down, George,' Moone said. 'He must be here somewhere.'

George turned his head and stared towards the door. A look seemed to come over his face, his eyes widening as he lifted a trembling finger and pointed at the door. 'He's out there. He's gone out there.'

'No one's gone out,' Butler said and stepped over to him. 'He'll be in the pub somewhere. We'll find him.'

George shook his head. 'No. He's out there. I've got to look for him.'

The old man went to move towards the door, but Moone and Butler blocked his way.

'No one's going out there, George,' Butler said

firmly.

The old man looked ready to argue, his lower lip trembling, but the fight seemed to drain out of him. He turned back to his table and sat down heavily, muttering something under his breath.

Then the lights flickered again. Once. Twice.

And went out once more.

A collective groan rippled through the room, followed by nervous laughter. Someone knocked a glass over. The fire, still burning strong, threw enough light to paint everyone in shades of orange and black.

Maggie's voice rose over the muttering as she said, 'Bloody thing's been playing up for months. Someone'll have to go down the back and check the fuse box. There's a storeroom past the kitchen door, right before the back door. Fuse box is on the wall.'

No one moved. Moone observed them all in the flickering firelight, seeing their either indifferent or fearful expressions.

Butler huffed in the dark. 'I'll go, then.'

Moone stood up. 'No, I'll go.'

'You sure?' Butler asked. 'Want me to hold your hand?'

He laughed. 'No, I'll be fine, Mum. But I haven't got my phone.'

She shook her head, then pulled her phone from her pocket and handed it to him. 'Here.'

He nodded. 'Keep everyone here. No one goes outside.'

The phone's thin white beam cut through

the gloom, catching several faces that blinked and guarded their eyes as they complained. Moone headed behind the bar and through the narrow doorway that led to the back. The corridor beyond was colder, the wind whispering faintly through cracks in the old stone. The floorboards creaked underfoot. Great, he thought as he edged along, just when he thought the situation couldn't get any creepier. He moved slowly, shining the torch along the narrow passage. The walls were lined with old photos and hooks holding coats and aprons. The smell of damp and beer barrels mixed in the still air. Somewhere above there was a creak, a floorboard shifting, or a footstep. He stopped, holding his breath. It was nothing. Just an old pub settling down, and the wind making noises.

'The bloody fuse box,' he muttered to himself, his voice hollow in the darkness.

The wind howled outside. Somewhere in the distance, something metallic clattered. It could be a loose latch, or the pub sign again. He reached the end of the corridor and pushed open the storeroom door. It groaned on its hinges.

Inside, the phone's torchlight swept over crates of bottled cider, piles of wood stacked against the wall, a row of shelves filled with cleaning products and tools. The fuse box was ahead of him, half-hidden behind an old calendar.

As he took a step inside, something moved to his left. He froze, the torch jerking in his hand. A shadow shifted across the wall, tall, human-shaped.

His heart thumped. He aimed the light, and the shape loomed up before him.

A coat.

He breathed out, his heart still pounding.

It was only a coat hanging from a hook, swaying gently in the draught from the back door.

He let out a humourless laugh. 'Jesus, Moone, get a grip.'

He turned, moving the torchlight back across the room. The beam skimmed over the floor. Then he stopped.

Something was lying there.

There was a boot caught in the light.

Then he moved the light across the leg attached to the boot.

Moone stepped forward, the air seeming to thicken around him. The torchlight crept over the still form of a man sprawled on the cold stone floor, snow glistening on his coat. His flat cap was knocked askew, his eyes half open.

'Warren,' Moone whispered, his heart racing again.

The man didn't move. The phone trembled slightly in Moone's hand. His pulse hammered in his throat.

He crouched down slowly, his breath visible in the torchlight, swirling in the icy air. He reached for the man's neck. His skin was cold. There was no pulse.

'Bloody hell,' he muttered as he got to his feet. 'He's dead.'

THREE

Moone jumped when he heard a sound behind him. From somewhere in the dark, through the corridor, the wind moaned again. It was low and drawn out, like someone breathing in the dark.

He turned his head towards the sound, trembling all over, the light quivering on the wall.

He went to call for Butler but stopped. He didn't want to spend another second alone with a dead man in the dark, so he started moving, following the torchlight as he made his way out of the storeroom and out into the icy cold corridor. His breath plumed as he hurried back towards the firelight of the pub.

'Moone?' Butler called in the dark as he caught sight of her orange and red shape. 'Didn't you find the fuse box? Have you been faffing again?'

Moone passed by Maggie who was still behind the bar and edged his way to Butler.

'Something bad's happened,' he whispered to her.

'Something bad? Like what?'

'Warren. He's dead. I found him in the storeroom, lying on the floor.'

Silence came from Butler, but he could sense her eyes on him.

'Are you having me on?' she said finally.

'No, I wish I was. He's dead, lying on the storeroom floor.'

'Who's dead?' Hannah's strained voice came from the darkness.

'The lights are dead,' Butler said. 'Come on, Moone, I'll help. Afraid of the dark, this one. No one move, people.'

As they made their way along the cold, draughty corridor, the wind howling again, Butler said, 'This isn't the time to be joking, Pete.'

'I'm not,' he said, beaming the torchlight before them. 'On my mum's life…'

'Isn't your mum dead?'

'Well, yes, but you know what I mean. He's lying in there.'

The lights flickered on then off. Then the corridor lit up, the fluorescent light above them flashing to life. Moone turned off the phone's light as he said, 'Well, that's fixed that.'

Butler eyed him suspiciously, then gave a deep huff before she hurried on down the corridor and stopped in the doorway of the storeroom. Moone could see her eyes were fixed on the floor.

'See, I told you,' he said, catching up. When he stood next to her, his eyes found the stone floor. But Warren was not lying dead there. In fact, Moone was surprised, confused and a little relieved, to find only a coat lying on the ground as if it had slipped from a coat hook.

A punch landed on his arm. He swung round to see Butler glaring at him.

'You're a wally, Moone,' she said, shaking her head. 'You had me going.'

He stepped into the room, rubbing his arm, staring at the spot where Warren had been. He hadn't imagined it. He knew he had touched his cold skin, had felt there was no pulse. He turned and stared at Butler.

'He was here,' he said. 'I swear. I don't like to say it and tempt fate, but on Alice's life, Warren was lying dead on the floor.'

Her eyes narrowed, then she looked towards the door. 'Well, if he was, where did he go?'

'I have no bloody idea.'

'More to the point, if he is dead, then who killed him? And why?'

Moone stepped closer, his mind rushing in all directions. 'You don't think the escaped prisoner is here?'

'No. He'll be miles away by now. Why would he come here?'

Moone shrugged. 'No idea. We'd better get back to the rest. What do we say?'

'Nothing. We keep schtum. There's no point starting a panic. Let's subtly find out where everyone was.'

'We know where they were. Everyone was in the pub, apart from George and Warren.'

'But the lights went out. Some bugger could've

sneaked off.'

He nodded. 'True. Well, let's ask some subtle questions.'

'Well, is someone dead?' Alma said, her dark eyebrows raised as they both stepped around the bar and stood at the centre of the pub.

'No, no one's dead,' Butler said, her voice calm. 'But has anyone seen Mr Warren?'

'Not since he went out for a ciggy,' John said, stifling a yawn. 'Don't tell me it's him who's dead? Told you, it's always the quiet ones.'

Butler turned and glared at him. 'That doesn't even make sense. If Warren turned out to be a murderer that would make sense. He's just missing, that's all.'

'Missing, presumed dead?' Alma said, standing up and putting her glass on the bar. 'Another please, Maggie.'

'Rusty,' the old man said, his hand on the blanket where his old dog had been lying. 'Where's Rusty? Has anyone seen him?'

Butler turned to Moone. 'Where is the dog?'

Moone shrugged and stepped further into the room. 'Right, has anyone seen Mr Warren or Rusty?'

'Maybe he took Rusty for a walk,' John said with a laugh.

'In this bloody weather?' Maggie said jabbing her finger towards the door.

'He went outside to smoke,' Hannah said.

'Warren or the dog?' John laughed.

Butler pointed at him. 'You are not bloody

funny.'

Then they all stopped talking as their collective eyes rose upwards. From above had come the creak of a floorboard. It was followed by another as if someone was making their way across the landing above.

'Who's up there?' Butler asked, staring at Maggie. But the landlady was looking perplexed up at the ceiling. She broke out of her stare and looked at Butler.

'Sorry, what?' Maggie said.

'Who's up there? Someone's moving around up there.'

Maggie shook her head. 'No one's up there. Warren's the only one staying. There shouldn't be anyone up there.'

George jumped to his feet like a man half his age, his eyes wide.

'Rusty!' he called, staring upwards. 'He must've wandered up there. Rusty! Come here, boy.'

The old man hurried past Moone and Butler and around the bar. Maggie blocked his way, her hands touching his elbows.

'All right, calm down, George,' she said. 'I'll go and take a look. If he's up there, I'll bring him down.'

'I don't think that's wise,' Butler said. 'I think one of us should take a look. We're police officers.'

'So you say,' John said. 'Got any proof of that?'

Butler produced a deep and particularly loud huff as she pulled her warrant card from her coat and held it out for John to see. 'That enough for you?'

He shrugged. 'Seems genuine.'

Butler turned to Moone. 'You keep an eye on this lot, I'll go take a look around up there.'

'You sure?'

Butler nodded as she reached into her other coat pocket and flashed him her Casco baton. 'Yeah, I'm sure. Just keep an eye on this lot while I'm gone.'

Butler tightened her grip on the Casco baton as she headed towards the narrow, bare wooden stairs. Each step creaked under her boots, the sound almost too loud in the stillness. She paused at the second step as she saw an old light switch on the wall, and flicked it. Nothing. She would have used her phone's torch but the battery was low.

'Bleeding great,' she sighed under her breath.

The landing above was swallowed in darkness, the faint glow from the corridor below barely reaching the first few steps. She could feel the draught moving down the stairwell, the iciness brushing past her, a ghostlike whisper across her face.

She shook her head as she tightened her coat. The whole night was turning into one big pain in the arse. This was the last time she was going anywhere with Moone just before Christmas. He was like one of those people you never took on a boat, a proper bad omen. Except Moone was bad luck wherever he went. If there was a quiet evening to be had, he'd find a way to drag trouble to it.

Her heart thudded as she climbed another few steps. She couldn't see much, but her eyes were adjusting, grey shapes beginning to form. There was the outline of the banister and the top step. The landing above gaped open like a black mouth. But there was no sign of George's dog.

'Rusty?' she called.

Nothing.

The wind whistled through the rafters, thin and eerie, like it was threading through cracks in the old roof.

At the top she hesitated, baton held ready. Through the gloom she could make out three doors facing her on the landing. One was slightly ajar, and a fourth, wider doorway at the end seemed to lead to a bathroom, she guessed, from the faint reflection she could see of herself in a mirror above a sink.

She stepped forward. The floorboards creaked and groaned under her weight. She tried the first door. Locked. The second was open.

The smell of stale air and tobacco hit her first, and then the faint scent of aftershave. She stepped inside, sweeping her eyes around the small, plain room. She tried the light switch on the wall. Nothing.

Her eyes had adjusted to the dark, allowing her to see a bed which was unmade. A small chest of drawers was beside it in a corner. A dark window sat at one end, and the wind whistled through a gap in the wooden frame. She turned her eyes back to the bed where a suitcase was lying open.

She frowned as she crossed to it. She looked back towards the door and out to the dark corridor. She shrugged and decided to give the case a quick rummage. All she found was some shirts, socks, a half bottle of whisky, and a pack of disposable razors. Then she spotted something tucked inside a side pocket. A passport.

She slipped it out and flipped it open. Warren's face stared back at her. Same nose, same eyes, same creased mouth, but the problem was, it was not his name printed inside it.

'James Kasper,' she read.

What the bloody hell was going on?

Her brow furrowed as she checked the date of birth, the country, the stamps. Everything about it looked real, all except the man who they had met downstairs, the man who was now missing, the man who Moone said had been lying dead on the storeroom floor, had not called himself James Kasper.

'Who the hell are you, Warren?' she whispered.

She slipped the passport into her coat pocket, unease creeping into her gut. Something was very wrong here. The storm, the convict, a missing man, the dead lights, a missing dog and now a fake identity.

She turned slowly, the shadows of the room seeming to close in, and stepped back onto the landing. The wind moaned through the roof again, colder now, the sound of it like a voice half-whispering her name.

For the first time that night, she wished she wasn't alone up there.

Then it hit her. Moone.

He was downstairs with all of them. Alone.

Her heart gave a hard thump against her ribs. She took the stairs two at a time, the old wood groaning under her boots as she hurried, the cold air chasing her, biting at her back all the way down into the darkness below.

The storm outside seemed to have quietened down to a low moan. The wind lightly rattled the windows rather than howling through them. The fire crackled, throwing long, restless shadows across the walls. George was sitting hunched in his chair, muttering to himself and staring into the flames. Every so often he whispered his dog's name: Rusty, Rusty, as if saying it might conjure the old hound back.

Moone felt sorry for him as he leaned against the bar, notebook in hand, his pen poised. Butler was upstairs looking around, while he was stuck with the rest. He kept seeing Warren lying lifeless on the floor. He hadn't imagined the whole thing, had not hallucinated feeling for his pulse. Something was going on here. It was time to start getting answers.

At that moment the lights flickered back on and cheers went up and a loud bang echoed through the pub. Moone instinctively ducked as if someone had fired a shot. Hannah screamed.

'Bloody tree lights,' John said and Moone straightened up and saw the lights on the Christmas tree in the corner had gone out.

'Holy shit,' Alma said, 'I nearly had a heart attack.'

So did I, thought Moone.

'Ho ho ho,' John said.

'All right,' Moone said, glancing around the room. 'Let's make this quick. Since we're all stuck here for the foreseeable future, or until the blizzard stops, I want to know who I'm sharing a roof with. So… who's first?' He looked at John. 'Why don't we start with you?'

John looked up slowly, his mouth twisting into that half-smile Moone already disliked. 'What is this, an interrogation?'

'It's just a chat,' Moone said, putting on a smile. 'Let's start with your name, what you do, and what brings you to Dartmoor tonight.'

John sighed, set down his mug and said, 'I'm John, you know that. And I'm a man who earns a lot more than you do as a police officer, DCI.'

'Good for you,' Moone said. 'John what?'

'John Ryland.'

'What line of work do you earn all this money in, John?'

There was a small silence. Then, reluctantly he said, 'I'm a solicitor.'

'And you're on your way to Plymouth, you

said?'

John nodded. 'Client meeting. Business. And before you start asking, anything else is none of your business.'

Moone jotted it all down, unfazed. 'Right.' He looked up, about to move on, when Alma straightened in her seat, crossing one long leg over the other.

'What about you, Alma?'

She tilted her head, lips curving. 'Can't you tell what I am, Peter? Just from looking at me?'

'It's DCI Moone,' he said dryly. 'And no, I can't tell. Why don't you tell me?'

'I'm a model.' She gave a little pose, her red lips curling into a smile. 'If we're being crass and talking money, I bet I make a lot more than John here.'

John gave a short laugh. 'I get it,' he said, nodding. 'You're on that site. OnlyFans. Yeah, I bet you make loads on there, flashing your bits to strangers.'

Alma's smile didn't falter. 'If you've got it, flaunt it. Isn't that right, Peter?'

Moone met her gaze, kept himself stone-faced. 'Why are you in Plymouth, Alma?'

'It's where I grew up,' she said, voice softening a little. 'Visiting my family for Christmas.'

John laughed, leaning back. 'Do they know you flash your bits for a living?'

'That's enough,' Moone said, trying to put some authority in his voice. He looked at Alma again. 'Surname?'

'Wilson. Alma Wild-One I'm known as online.'

The room went still for a moment. The wind outside sighed through the old chimney while the flames danced wildly.

Moone turned his attention to the young couple sitting near the fire. Hannah looked nervous; Tom had that permanent scowl that made him seem older than he was.

'What about you two?' Moone asked, pen ready again. 'Surnames?'

Hannah sat up, smiling nervously. 'Hannah Pollard. Tom Hocking.'

'I can talk for myself,' Tom said.

'Sorry.' Hannah blushed and looked down at her hands.

'So why are you here?' Moone asked, fighting the urge to clip Tom round the ear.

'I'm visiting Hannah,' Tom muttered. 'She's a student.'

'Marjons,' she said quietly.

'How come you ended up here?'

'We were on our way to Tavistock. My mum lives there. The roads were already bad, so we thought we'd stop here when we saw the lights. Maggie said we could stay until morning.'

Tom didn't look up. 'We've got nothing to do with any of this,' he said flatly. 'We're just trying to get home.'

Moone studied him for a second. The kid's leg was bouncing, fast and nervous.

'Relax, Tom,' Moone said quietly. 'Nobody's

accusing you of anything. Not yet.'

Tom finally looked up, his eyes cold. 'Then maybe you should stop asking questions like we're all suspects.'

Maggie cleared her throat and said, 'George is a local before you ask. He lives a few streets away.'

Moone made more notes, then looked at Maggie. 'Do you know what Warren does for a living?'

'His name isn't Warren,' Butler said, appearing through the door. She had a passport in her hand as she came round the bar to Moone. 'His name is James Kasper. But I'm not sure what he did for a living or what he was doing here.'

Moone took the passport and flipped through it. Then he looked up. 'What the hell's going on?' he whispered. 'Why did someone kill him?'

'Did they? There's no body.'

Moone looked her in the eyes. 'There was. I didn't imagine it.'

'All right. Well, what's next?'

Moone glanced around the room, at Alma's smile, John's smirk, Tom's scowl, and Hannah's anxious eyes.

Something was not right. The tension was heavy in the air, and every face here had something to hide. He could feel it.

'Who's that out there?' Alma said. Moone had hardly noticed that she had got up and was looking out the window.

John got up and joined her. 'Who? I can't see

anyone.'

Alma tapped a long nail on the glass. 'There's a figure. He's standing out there, watching us. Can't you see him?'

Moone moved closer as John said, 'Oh, yes, I can. What the hell is he doing out there?'

'Let me take a look,' Moone said to John, who glared at him and reluctantly moved out of the way.

He bent over towards the window beside Alma. As her perfume clawed at his face, he stared in the gloom, where myriad snowflakes were being blown around. All he could make out was the darkness. 'I can't see anything.'

'You need your eyes tested,' Alma said, pointing at the glass again. 'There. Look.'

Moone squinted into the white and black blur where she was pointing. A faint light glowed in the window of one of the village houses, a small, steady pulse in the dark. Between it and the pub he thought he saw something else, a shape jutting from the ground. It looked like a thick post, tall and weathered, now half buried by the snow.

It was hard to make anything out; the falling snow distorted everything like static on a broken television screen desperately searching for a signal.

Then something moved.

A figure, or what looked like one, stepped away from the post.

Moone blinked, leaning forward, his breath fogging the glass. For a moment he thought his eyes were playing tricks on him, the snow and darkness conspiring to invent ghosts. He stared, his heart thudding.

The post was still there, but the figure, whatever it had been, was gone.

FOUR

'So what was it?' Butler asked as Moone stepped back from the window, scratching his head.

'Just the snow and the dark,' he said, and heard the doubt in his own voice.

'Someone's out there,' Alma said and downed the rest of her gin and tonic.

Butler pointed at her. 'I'm surprised you're not seeing fairies the way you're putting them away.'

'I've been drinking tea all evening and I saw it,' John said, leaning back in his chair, eyebrows raised.

'It's him,' George said, staring down at his hands.

'It's who?' Butler asked and stepped closer to him.

He looked up, staring, his bloodshot eyes a little wet. 'Hood. Joseph Hood. He said he'd come back for revenge.'

'I'm sorry, George,' she said and huffed. 'But that's just some old wives' tale. Either someone's lost out there, probably Warren or whoever he really is, or everyone's started seeing things. My money's on the possibility that you've all gone mad.'

'Where's Rusty?' George said, staring pleadingly up at Butler. 'He could be out there freezing.'

'Well, he's not upstairs,' Butler said, and looked at Moone and rolled her eyes.

Moone sighed, then looked towards the main door that rattled and whistled as the wind tried to get into the warm.

'I'll go and take a look,' he said, half hoping his offer would be met with protest.

'Someone needs to stay with this lot,' Butler whispered. 'Or I'd come with you.'

He let out a heavy sigh and started to button up his coat.

'Is that all you've brought with you?' John said, tutting and getting up out of the leather chair. 'I thought you police officers were supposed to be prepared. You'd better take my coat, it's thick and warm.'

Moone raised his eyebrows as he watched the arrogant solicitor pick up a thick coat that had been lying folded on the table and hand it to him.

'It's also very expensive,' John said. 'So do bring it back or I'll sue you.'

Moone flashed a smile full of sarcasm as he took off his coat and slipped on John's. He instantly felt much warmer.

'Thanks,' he said.

'Here, take this,' Butler said and held out her phone, then her Casco baton. 'Just in case. Not much battery left on the phone though.'

'Oh, I've got these,' Maggie said as she ducked behind the bar. She came up red-faced and holding some pepper spray in one hand and a baseball bat in the other.

'A baseball bat and pepper spray?' Butler said, staring at the landlady. 'You get a lot of trouble out here, do you?'

'Well, no, but you can never be too careful.' Maggie looked awkward.

Moone took hold of the pepper spray as he said, 'Well, seeing as pepper spray is a prohibited weapon under the Firearms Act 1968 and is illegal to own, sell, or carry in public, I'll confiscate it. It might come in handy though. Thanks.'

'You're very welcome,' Maggie said. 'I'll tell you what, I'll put some food on for when you get back. I've got some sausage rolls in the freezer.'

Moone smiled. 'Thanks.'

'Good luck,' Alma said, and winked at him.

'Thanks.' Moone headed to the door and opened it. Immediately the wind attacked the door, threatening to rip it off its hinges. He grabbed the handle as it rattled. He fought to push it open as a cloud of snow was sprayed into his face.

'Rusty!' George shouted as he barged past Moone and rushed out into the darkness.

Moone cursed under his breath and went after him. 'George! Wait!'

The wind hit him like a wall as he left the warmth of the pub. The door slammed behind him, cutting off the pub's light. He was instantly swallowed by the storm, the icy snow whipping at his face, stinging his eyes, and blinding him. He lifted Butler's phone but the torchlight flickered weakly, a dull beam against the chaos. He raised his arm to guard his face so he could try to see something, anything.

'George!' he called out, his voice ripped away by the wind.

Nothing.

The world was white noise. Snow screamed sideways, the air thick with it, his breath fizzling off into the night. As Moone started walking, his boots crunched deep into the snow, still half blind, feeling stupid and mad for following. All he could make out was faint outlines ahead, the shapes of cottages, the low stone wall of the churchyard, and the faint yellow glow from a single house window. Somewhere between that solitary light and the dark shape of the pub, the old hanging post was standing, a thick silhouette reaching up in the turbulent air. He'd seen it earlier from the window of the pub, but now it loomed taller, black against the storm, leaning slightly, the rope gone but the hook still there.

The snow spun around him, disorienting him, almost blotting out the world. He turned, trying to get his bearings, but the storm had swallowed everything. He couldn't even see his own footprints any more.

'George!' he shouted again as he cupped his hands round his mouth. He shouted again but louder this time. His voice came back at him in fragments, broken by the wind.

Then, faintly, he heard it. He listened again. Yes, a bark. A single, desperate sound carried through the storm. Rusty.

'George! Rusty! Rusty! Come here, boy!'

He moved towards the sound, the snow biting his face, his legs getting heavier and heavier. Shadows shifted all around him, shapes moving against the white, dissolving before he had a chance to focus. His heart hammered. He blinked the ice from his lashes, convinced something was there with him.

Then it was gone and there was only snow and silence.

He stopped, gasping, the air burning in his lungs, making his chest ache. He knew if he kept going, he'd get lost. He turned, searching for the lights of the Scurry Inn. They were there, but only faint as if he had walked miles. But it was his only anchor.

He started back, head bowed, the wind shoving him sideways. Then something moved at the edge of his vision.

He stopped dead.

The hanging post.

He was close now, closer than he'd realised and much closer than he wanted to be. He raised Butler's phone and the beam of the torch caught it. There was the rough timber all black with age, snow clinging to its surface.

But it looked different somehow.

Then with a bolt of fear in his chest he saw why.

A shape was hanging from it.

His chest tightened. 'Oh, Jesus Christ...'

He stepped closer, each step heavy, his stomach turning, his heart thumping. The wind hissed around him, the snow swirling like ash. He raised the torch.

It was George.

The old man's boots swung inches from the ground, his head bowed, his body motionless as the snow gripped his skin. The rope creaked faintly above him, half frozen.

'Jesus, no...' Moone reached up, tried to lift him, his hands slipping on the icy rope. He wrapped his arms around George's waist and tried to heave him up but the old man's weight was dead and heavy. His face was grey, his mouth open, as if trying to speak.

'George...'

Moone let go of him and put a hand on his chest. There was no movement. No wisps of breath escaped his lips. The only sound was the groaning wind and the creak of the rope.

Moone stepped back, chest heaving, staring up at the old man.

For a heartbeat, he thought he saw George's eyes move. He blinked hard. Nothing.

Just the storm.

He turned and stumbled back towards the pub, snow clawing at his eyes, his hands trembling. His breath came in short bursts, clouds of white filling his vision.

Moone didn't look back as he ran towards the lights of the pub. The door was closed when he reached it so he hammered on it.

It was Butler who pulled it open, looking concerned as the snow blasted into her face. 'What's wrong? Did you see Warren or the dog?'

Moone pointed back towards the hanging post. 'It's George. He's dead. I found him hanging.'

Butler looked out into the darkness and the swirl of snow that made it hard to make out anything but shapes. 'You're joking? Where?'

'I need to get him down!' Moone noticed Tom had turned to face him, showing a little more interest. 'Tom! Come and help me. Someone grab a knife!'

'Here!' Maggie called out and came round the bar holding out a small kitchen knife. Moone took it. Tom was slowly putting on his coat as if it weighed the same as the pub itself.

'Come on, hurry up!' Moone ordered, then turned back to the storm and the haze of white that touched and bit into his skin. He forced himself on, shining the phone's light and trying to spot the silhouette of the hanging post. All there was, was the light of the house and the constant snowy static and wind that screeched in his ears. The wind kept pushing him back. He turned and caught Tom hurrying to keep up, his head down.

Then it appeared again, that black, thick and tall beacon of death against the dull light of the village. The wind came blasting in, the snow blinding him again as he got closer. He blinked and looked up.

'Where is it?' Tom shouted behind him, his voice breaking up.

Moone ignored him as he was staring at the hanging post where there was no body hanging. Certainly, there was no George. He looked around at the snow-laden ground, the dark buildings broken up by the flurries of snow. He looked down at the ground, looking for footprints but only saw his own and Tom's going to and from the pub.

'What the bloody hell's going on?' he moaned.

'Can we get back in the bloody warm?' Tom was hunched in his coat, hands stuffed in his pockets, hopping from one foot to the other. His pale skin was scarlet around his cheeks and nose.

Shit. Moone spun round, half expecting to see someone staring and laughing at him. There was nothing and no one.

'Come on,' he said and started trudging back towards the pub, Tom hurrying behind.

When they reached the door, Moone told the lad to go on in and get warm, while he stood vigil for a moment, staring back towards the post. He didn't know if it was the cold, the snow or instinct, but an icy feeling was crawling over his back, telling him something very wrong was going on. He got that old bite at the back of his throat, the shaky desire for a cigarette. He wondered if there might be a pack in the coat John had lent him. He put his hands in the pockets. There were no cigarettes, but he felt a rectangular piece of hard plastic. He pulled it out. His eyes widened and his gut became even more twisted when he saw it was a visitor pass for Channings Wood Prison.

What the hell? He put the card back into the pocket before he headed into the pub and firmly bolted the door behind him.

'So?' Butler was staring at him, eyes wide, eyebrows rising up her forehead.

He shook his head, then took off the coat, his eyes falling on John.

'What does that mean?' Butler said, following him as he held the coat out to the solicitor who was now standing.

'Thanks,' Moone said.

'Anytime,' John said. 'So, where's the body?'

'Yeah, where's the body?' Butler asked.

'There's no fucking body,' Tom grumbled as he took off his coat and slumped back into his seat. 'It was a waste of time.'

'Tom, don't,' Hannah said, quietly.

'He's right,' Moone said, noticing all eyes were on him. 'I went back and there was no body. Someone took it down.'

John leaned back and scoffed. 'Are you sure, my friend? Maybe the weather's playing tricks on you. Or maybe it's the spirit of Joseph Hood. Out there calling for his beloved wife. Mary! Mary! Please, forgive me, I didn't do it!'

Butler stepped over to him, folding her arms.

'Well, you seem to know quite a bit about Joseph Hood. How come?'

He stared at her, then glanced around the room, where everyone else was peering back at him. He nodded and sat up straight. 'Fair enough. You caught me out. OK, cards on the table.'

'Go on,' Butler said, leaning against the bar. 'This should be interesting.'

Moone kept a careful eye on the so-called solicitor as he leaned back in his chair, looking far too relaxed. 'The real reason I'm down this way is because I'm looking into a little family history for a client.'

'Who's your client?' Moone asked.

'That's confidential. But I can tell you that it involves this village. Hence why I'm here.'

Moone exchanged looks with Butler and it was clear she didn't believe him either.

'Have you found out anything interesting?' Moone asked, folding his arms.

John nodded and sat forward. 'Turns out he's related to Joseph Hood. In fact, he might be his only living relative.'

'And you happen to be here on the anniversary of his hanging?' Butler huffed.

But the solicitor shrugged. 'Pure coincidence. I had no idea. Anyway, that's why I'm here. Believe me, or choose not to.'

'Food's up!' Maggie called out. 'Hot sausage rolls. And cheese and onion ones for any veggies.'

Moone turned to see the landlady carrying two

large plates of sausage rolls. The smell found his nostrils and his stomach grumbled. With all the excitement, he hadn't had a chance to think about food.

'Be a love,' Maggie said to him as she held out a cup of coffee. 'Pass that to the young woman.'

Moone took the coffee and turned to find Alma smiling at him, sitting with her legs crossed. He put the coffee down in front of her and nodded.

'Thank you, kind sir,' she said.

Moone backed away and decided to rest his back against the bar, observing the scene. Butler was holding her phone up, trying to get a signal.

'Sausage rolls,' John said, moving between him and Butler. 'I can't say no to them.'

'Get me one,' Alma called out.

John huffed but grabbed a couple of sausage rolls and passed one to Alma.

'Moone,' Butler said, sliding beside him and giving him a dig. 'A word in the hallway.'

He nodded and followed her. When she stopped and faced him, arms folded, he said, 'I know what you're going to say, but I really did see George hanging…'

'Shut up, you wally,' she said, her eyes darting towards the bar. 'It's not about that. It's about Alma and John.'

Moone looked over his shoulder and caught a glimpse of John munching away. 'What about them?'

'They know each other.' She stared at him.

'Where'd you get that from?'

'A sausage roll told me.'

'What?'

'Alma asked John to get her a sausage roll, right? I watched what he did. He grabbed a meat one for himself and a veggie one for her. How did he know she'd want a cheese one?'

Moone shrugged. 'Maybe... he just randomly grabbed one.'

'No. Not only that. When he passed her the cheese and onion roll, she didn't say thank you.'

'So, she doesn't seem to like him.'

'When someone you hardly know passes you something, you say thanks. When your other half hands you something, you don't say a thing.'

'Really?'

'Trust me. They know each other.'

Moone turned towards the pub where he could now hear some light chatter. 'It's funny you should say that because I discovered something interesting.'

'What? Come on, don't faff.'

'Before I came back in from the cold, I had a cheeky look in John's coat pockets.'

She huffed. 'You were looking for a fag, weren't you?'

He laughed. 'Anyway, I found a visitor pass from Channings Wood Prison.'

Butler raised her eyes, staring past Moone. 'Bloody Nora. What is it with this lot? But what do we do? We've got no bodies, nothing. Just two missing people who could easily be lost in a storm…'

'Apart from the fact I saw them both dead.'

Butler sighed. 'We've got no signal, so it's not like we can look any of them up. Unless Maggie has a landline and we call Harding or Chambers.'

FIVE

DC Keith Harding stirred, frowning as something nudged his shoulder. For a second he thought it was part of the dream he'd been having that was quickly fading, but the nudging came again, harder this time.

He opened one bleary eye and saw the room was dark, the glow from the streetlights outside shining through the curtains. Tia was leaning over him, her face close, eyes narrowed in that familiar look that told him he'd done something wrong.

'What now?' he mumbled, his voice rough. He cleared his throat and blinked up at her.

She was holding out his phone. 'Someone's calling. Middle of the bloody night. You're lucky they didn't wake Jake.'

'Sorry,' he muttered, sitting up and rubbing his eyes. He took the phone from her hand, blinking at the screen, not recognising the number.

'This better be good,' he said as he answered.

'Oi, you cheeky bastard,' came Butler's voice down the line, the huff hovering somewhere in it.

Harding shot upright, almost out of bed. 'Sorry,

Mand... I mean, sorry, boss.'

He could hear her sigh on the other end. 'Forget it. Sorry if I woke your house, but we've got trouble.'

'Trouble?' He swung his legs out of bed and tried to find his slippers. 'What trouble? Where are you?'

'Snowed in,' Butler said. Her voice crackled slightly, like the line was hanging by a thread. 'We're in some little village in Dartmoor.'

Harding rubbed his face, trying to wake himself as he stood up. He wandered to the window, and pulled the curtain aside. Outside, the Barbican sat quiet and still. The harbour lights blinked, the sea beyond invisible in the dark. Only a light dusting of snow drifted down, glowing amber under the street lamps.

'Hardly any snow here,' he said.

'Why doesn't that surprise me?' she replied. 'Listen, we've got no signal where we are, so we need you to look up some people for us.'

He gave a tired grunt. 'Right, hang on. Let me find my bleeding notebook.'

He stepped across the room, opening a drawer as quietly as he could so as not to wake the rest of the flat. Behind him, Tia groaned and rolled over, pulling the duvet over her.

'You owe me a lie-in, Keith,' she muttered and turned over.

Harding smiled, then grabbed his notepad and pen and headed to the kitchen and sat on a chair. 'Go on then,' he said, flipping it open. 'Who are we looking for this time?'

Moone leaned back against the wall as Butler read out the names to Harding. They were both standing upstairs in a small lounge area at the back of the pub. The room had a large TV, a battered leather sofa and the phone. He was busy thinking, trying to fathom what was going on, trying to work out why someone would murder two people and then make them disappear. He thought of the escaped prisoner, Raymond Keel, who was more than likely out there somewhere.

'Ask him to find out about Keel,' Moone said, stepping away from the wall.

Butler stared at him. 'Who?'

'The escaped prisoner.'

She nodded. 'Did you hear that, Keith? Moone wants you to find out about Raymond Keel who escaped from prison tonight… anything about him. Got it? All right, call us back on this number when you've got anything interesting. Talk soon.'

Butler hung up and sighed as she faced Moone. 'Keith is on it.'

Moone nodded, his eyes jumping to the floor where there seemed to be some raised voices in the bar below. Then he heard a thump.

'What the hell was that?'

Another thump came from below, louder this time, a heavy, dull sound against the main door. It was followed by a muffled shout.

Moone and Butler stared at each other.

'That's not the bloody wind,' Butler said quietly.

They both moved, hurrying down the narrow stairs, their shoes thudding on the old wood. The sound came again from down in the pub, someone hammering at the door. The low, angry moan of the storm followed it, shaking the windows in their frames.

By the time Moone and Butler reached the bar, everyone was on their feet. Maggie was standing behind the counter, white-faced. Hannah was nearest the door, hovering uncertainly. Tom had a hand on her arm, trying to pull her back. John was clutching a bar stool by the legs, ready to swing it like a weapon. Alma was sitting on a stool by the bar, swirling the last of her gin lazily, her lipstick smudged but her smile still there.

'Someone's out there,' Hannah said, her voice breaking up. 'They're banging on the door!'

Moone flinched as the knocking started again, a fist being pounded on the door.

'Anyone in there?!' a muffled voice shouted, almost drowned out by the wind.

'Could be the escaped prisoner,' John said, raising the stool up over his shoulder. 'Leave it shut.'

'We can't just leave someone out there to freeze,' Hannah said, her eyes jumping to Moone. 'We can't, can we?'

'Might be some nutter,' Tom said. He was still sat on his stool, but had turned to stare at the door.

Alma lifted her glass, her eyes glassy and full of

amusement. 'Oh, let them in,' she said. 'Might liven the place up. It's boring me to death in here.'

John glared at her. 'You really are something else, you know that? Do you want to let in an escaped psycho?'

'From Channings Wood, you mean?' Moone stared at him, and saw John fix his eyes on him, a strange expression on his face.

'Why'd you say that?' John said.

Moone shook his head and stepped forward. 'Forget it. It's been a long day. All right, everyone calm down.'

He glanced at Butler. 'What do you think?'

Another shout came through the door. Muffled, panicked. 'Let me in! Please! Let me in! It's bloody freezing out here!'

The wind howled around it, turning the words into an almost ghostly echo.

Everyone became quiet.

'Well, we're all about preservation of life, so we can't ignore that,' Butler said, drawing her Casco baton. 'Whoever he is, we can't let him freeze out there.'

'Or let him kill us in here,' John growled. 'Are you mad?'

'Stand back,' Moone ordered. He moved towards the door, feeling the wind rattling it. 'If it's him, we'll deal with it. Get ready.'

John tightened his grip on the stool. 'If it's him, I'll deal with it.'

Butler stepped up beside Moone, baton ready.

The firelight behind them threw long, flickering shadows over the walls and the door. Everyone else had gone still, holding their breath.

Moone reached for the bolt, then he hesitated. The wood vibrated as another thump came from outside. It went right through his body and seemed to finish at his heart. He glanced at Butler.

She gave a short nod. 'Do it. Don't faff.'

Moone slid the bolt back.

The door flew open, the wind slamming it wide, a blast of icy air and snow exploding into the room. The lights flickered as the blizzard howled in.

Moone blinked as he wiped snow from his face.

In the doorway stood a man, thickset and broad-shouldered. He was wearing a dark raincoat crusted white with snow. His hair was dark too with a few streaks of grey; his face rough and raw from the cold. For a heartbeat he didn't move, no one moved, they were all standing there while the white storm raged.

Then the new arrival took a few steps forward. Everyone else stepped back, all eyes on him. Butler had her baton poised, while John lifted the stool even higher.

Moone stepped between the gang and the man. 'Easy. Let's see who we've got here.'

The man looked dazed as he glanced around. He was breathing hard as melting snow trickled down his face.

'Thank God,' he gasped. 'Thank God someone's here...'

Moone stared at him, watching the man starting to take off his coat. As Moone forced the door shut, a chill crawled up his spine that had nothing to do with the snow.

'Who are you?' Butler asked as the man went over to the fire to warm his hands.

The man swallowed hard as he rubbed his hands then brushed the snow from his hair. 'My name's Thurston. Ben. You two look like you're on the job.'

Moone looked at Butler who huffed and put down the baton on the bar. 'We are. The baton gives it away a bit, I guess.'

Thurston nodded and turned his back on the fire, his eyes still taking everyone in. 'I suppose it does. But you two have police stamped all over you. If you were sticks of rock, we could crack you open and you'd have copper running through you.'

'I bet you'd love to crack them open, wouldn't you?' John said, the stool still gripped in his hands.

The newcomer frowned at him. 'What does that mean?'

'Are you sure your name's not Keel?' John said.

Thurston laughed. 'I get it. He escaped tonight, I know. I was on my way home and I was going to check on some of his relatives that live a couple of miles from here. But my car got stuck. I had to leave it. God knows how far I've walked.'

'You work at the prison?' Moone asked, the coldness still gripping his backbone.

'No, I'm on the job like you two. I'm a DS. I was

just there looking into his escape. They reckon he had help on the inside.'

'Got any ID to prove that?' Butler asked. 'Where's your warrant card?'

Thurston let out a breath that was half a laugh. 'In the car. Glove box. Didn't think I'd need it.'

The room fell silent.

'Is there something going on here?' he said, his brow furrowing. 'Or are you lot just really paranoid?'

There came a drumroll played on the bar. Everyone looked over and saw Alma had her eyes wide, a smile on her lips. 'There's been… a murder. Actually, two murders.'

'You're kidding?' Thurston said, staring at Moone. 'Has there?'

'Actually, two missing, presumed dead.'

'Out there?' He pointed to the door.

Moone nodded. 'Yes, well, kind of.'

'They went out there but Moone saw them dead,' Butler said, folding her arms.

'You're Moone?' Thurston stared at him.

He nodded. 'That's right.'

'So two people went out there, then you saw them dead? Where?'

'Hang on a minute,' John said, putting down the stool with a thump. 'We still don't know who he really is. Where's your phone? There'll be something on there to tell us if he's really a copper.'

Thurston nodded, then reached for his coat that he'd hung over the back of a chair. He patted his coat for a moment, then closed his eyes. 'Shit. It was in here. Either I've lost it out there or it's in my car.'

'Convenient,' John said, and retreated to his chair.

'Well, why don't you have a drink?' Maggie said, smiling, trying to lighten the mood. 'Beer? Coffee? Tea?'

'Tea,' Thurston replied. 'I'd better keep my wits about me.'

'Don't be like that,' Alma said. 'Join the party.'

He laughed. 'Tea will be fine. Can I sit down?'

Hannah looked up and saw he was pointing to her table. She nodded and smiled. The man sat down, his eyes falling on Tom. 'Are you two a couple?'

'Yeah,' Tom grunted, his eyes on the table.

Moone walked closer to the fire, thinking it all through, trying to size the man up. Everything about him did read copper, the way he walked and talked, but then he remembered the old adage; if not a copper, then a criminal, one of his superiors used to say. 'Have you met Keel?'

Thurston picked up a beer mat and turned it in his thick hands. 'Briefly. Had a chat. He wasn't that talkative.'

'What's he like?'

He shrugged. 'Comes across as a gentleman. Polite. He's not stupid. But get on the wrong side of him and all that politeness soon falls away. Underneath it all, he's a monster.'

'Tell me, Ben,' Alma said as she got up and swayed her hips over towards the fire. 'Are you a monster?'

He gave a laugh and shook his head. 'No, you've nothing to fear from me.'

She rolled her eyes. 'That's a shame.'

Moone watched as Thurston stared at her strangely, then shook his head before he looked at him again. 'We need to call this in.'

'We already have, clever clogs,' Butler said. 'We've got one of our team looking into it.'

'And what's he looking into exactly?' Thurston sat back as Maggie came round the bar and put a tea in front of him and stood back, listening.

'I'm afraid I can't discuss that with you. For all we know you could be Keel.'

He picked up his tea and nodded. 'True, I could be. But I'm not. You'll have to take my word for it.'

Butler stepped closer to him as she said, 'Well, our colleague's also going to be giving us the lowdown on Keel, including a detailed description, so if one of you lot is him, we'll soon find out.'

'Keel's a man, right?' Alma said with a laugh.

'Yeah, he's a man.' Butler looked over at her. 'You aren't hiding anything, are you?'

Alma patted herself down, then smirked. 'Oh no, I'm all woman. Want to feel?'

Butler huffed. 'No, you're all right.'

DC Keith Harding stifled a yawn as the lights flickered on above him, bathing the incident room in its cold, artificial glow. He looked at his phone. It was nearly one a.m. He rubbed his neck and looked around him. The building felt hollow at this hour and so quiet. He could even hear the distant rumble of the heating pipes, the faint hum of the vending machine. Then somewhere far off, a door shutting with a soft echo.

Chambers came in, her dark hair tied up, her coat still on, carrying two steaming takeaway cups. She placed one on his desk.

'Thought you'd need this,' she said. 'A coffee with love from Jake's.'

Harding looked up at her, smiling. 'You're an angel.'

She smirked. 'Yeah, right. I don't feel like it right about now. Didn't even have time to put any makeup on.'

'You look fine. Anyway, we've got work to do.' He took a long sip as she perched on the corner of his desk. Harding thought, not for the first time, that bringing Chambers in on this was the best decision he'd made all week. She was sharper, faster, and more methodical than he'd ever be. Not that he'd admit that to her, or anyone else for that matter. She had made DS before him, and now he'd had time to digest it, he realised there was a perfectly valid reason.

'So,' she said, glancing at his notebook. 'What exactly are we looking into at stupid o'clock in the morning?'

Harding flipped open his notebook, turning it

67

towards her. His scrawled handwriting filled the page, a list of names underlined and numbered.

'That's what Moone and Butler called and gave me,' he said, stifling another yawn.

Chambers leaned over the desk, reading. 'John Ryland. Alma Wilson. Hannah Pollard. Tom Hocking. Warren…' She frowned and looked at Harding. 'Or James Kasper?'

'Yeah, he booked into the pub under the name Warren, but they found a passport in the name of James Kasper. Interesting, isn't it?'

'It is. And the landlady of the pub's called Maggie. All of them snowed in?'

'Yep,' Harding said, leaning back in his chair. 'Moone and Butler are stuck with them in some pub out on Dartmoor. The Scurry Inn.'

She blinked. 'That sounds like the start of a bad joke.'

'It gets better,' Harding said. 'Two of 'em are missing. Warren, or Kasper, and an old fella called George, and his dog. Moone reckons Warren was dead one minute and gone the next. Same with George. Butler's not sure what to believe. Could be the escaped prisoner they mentioned on the radio. Raymond Keel.'

'Keel?' she said, pulling up a chair opposite. 'What would he be doing there? If he's escaped, why hang around a pub in the middle of nowhere?'

Harding shrugged. 'Search me. Maybe the storm caught him out. Maybe he's taking refuge. Maybe he's got other plans. But Moone didn't sound too convinced it was a coincidence.'

Chambers frowned as she took a sip of her coffee, then stood and went to her desk. She started tapping away at her keyboard, the glow of the screen lighting her face. Harding watched her for a moment, impressed at how fast she could wake up when there was work to be done.

'What're you looking for?' he asked.

'The Scurry Inn,' she said. 'Trying to see if I can find anything on the place. Maybe there's some history to it.'

'You think it's haunted?' Harding said, smirking.

'Very funny.' She clicked through a few pages, then stopped. 'Well, this is interesting.'

'Go on, let's hear it.'

'Apparently,' she said, reading, 'the Scurry Inn is built near the site where a local man was hanged in the early 1800s. Joseph Hood. Accused of murdering a young woman. Swore he'd come back for revenge before they strung him up.'

Harding gave a low whistle. 'That's a cheery story.'

'Locals still talk about it,' Chambers went on, scrolling. 'Every couple of years, someone claims to see him wandering the village in the snow. Gives the place a bit of a reputation.'

Harding laughed as he sat back in his chair, picking up his coffee. 'What's the betting Moone and Butler have already had someone bring that up tonight?'

'Knowing their luck, probably.'

Harding had a cheeky thought and decided to share it. 'Hey, if those two are stuck out there in a pub in the middle of nowhere, maybe sat in front of a roaring fire… maybe they'll finally, you know?'

Chambers sighed. 'I wish. Anyone can see they've got eyes for each other. Although, what would happen about work if they did get together?'

Harding shrugged. 'I don't know. I suppose we should be worrying about getting them out of there. You don't actually think this Hood bloke's the one doing the murdering, do you?' Harding grinned.

Chambers looked over at him. 'No, course not, but I do think it's a bit weird. Especially if people are disappearing. It's just eerie.'

Harding laughed again, shaking his head. 'You've been watching too many ghost stories. Trust me, it won't be Hood doing the killing. It'll be someone with a pulse and bad intentions. Like Keel.'

'They haven't found him yet, then?'

Harding sipped his coffee as he looked at the information on his screen, a long list of despicable and downright evil behaviour. 'Nah, I don't think anyone's looking for him in this weather… hang on a minute.'

'What is it?' Chambers stood up and came over.

'Says here that his last visitor was a solicitor called Jack Ryman.'

'Prisoners are always getting visits from solicitors.'

'Yeah, true but look at the name of the solicitor

in the pub.'

He pushed the notebook over to her. Her eyes widened as she looked up. 'John Ryland. Same initials. What's going on?'

'I don't know but I'd better warn them. If this solicitor's got links to Keel, then God knows what's going on.'

SIX

'Maybe we shouldn't be just sitting around here,' Thurston said with a huff worthy of Butler on a bad day. He seemed to look everyone over intently as he got up from the table. 'If there are two missing persons out there, maybe we should be looking for them.'

Moone watched the man who said he was a policeman, examined the way he carried himself, the way his deep-set eyes read everyone in the room. 'There's no point,' Moone said. 'They're dead.'

He nodded, turning his eyes on Moone. 'Oh, yeah, we never got to the bottom of that. Didn't you say you saw them dead?'

Moone rubbed his eyes, ran his hands down his face, preparing to look foolish again. 'I went to check the fuse in the storage room and I found him. Warren. Or whoever he is…'

'What do you mean?' Thurston asked, coming round the table, his eyes digging into Moone.

'Butler found Warren's passport in his suitcase, in his room. It said he was James Kasper.'

Thurston narrowed his eyes. 'James Kasper? I

know that name. Where do I know that name from?'

'Maybe you two were good friends,' John said and gave a short laugh.

Thurston looked over at him. 'What about you? What's your story?'

'My story?' John sat back in his chair, steepling his fingers. 'Why I'm here? OK, I'll go over it again. My name is John Ryland. I'm a solicitor... look me up online... oh no, you can't can you? No signal.'

Thurston stepped closer. 'Why are you here?'

'Research for a client. It's confidential. I could tell you... but then I'd have to kill you.' John grinned, pleased with himself.

'You're hilarious, aren't you? I've not met many hilarious solicitors.'

'You should hang out here more often,' Alma said, lifting another gin and tonic to her lips. 'It's a riot. Shame we haven't got a karaoke machine, we could sing that song, what's it called? It's cold outside?'

'Baby, it's cold outside,' Moone corrected.

'I know, but I like the way you call me baby.' She raised one eyebrow as she smirked.

Moone turned away, thinking it all through, trying to make sense of it all. Nothing made sense. All he knew was that they were stuck in a storm, snowed in with a murderer on the loose.

'Well, I'm going to take a look outside,' Thurston said and headed for his coat.

'I don't think that's very bloody wise,' Butler said, arms folded.

With one hand on his coat, he turned and stared at her. 'Why? Because it's a bit chilly outside?'

'No, because two people are dead, or missing, and the last thing we need is another. I think we should all stay here.'

'Where you two can keep an eye on us?' John said. 'So we don't kill anyone, am I right?'

'Can anyone hear that?' Hannah said, sitting bolt upright.

'What?' Butler asked.

'Oh, it's the phone.' Maggie pointed upwards.

Moone hurried around the bar and along the corridor, then up the stairs with Butler not far behind.

'Nobody leaves!' Butler barked as she reached the stairs.

Moone grabbed the phone and lifted it to his ear. There was heavy breathing on the other end. 'Who is this?'

'It's me, boss, Harding.' There was a laugh. 'Sorry, couldn't resist.'

'You're not funny. Got anything?'

'Yeah. Turns out Keel was visited by a solicitor not long before he escaped. Jack Ryman. Same initials as the guy you're stuck with. Bit weird, isn't it?'

Moone turned and saw Butler in the doorway, listening. 'That is weird. So a solicitor with the same initials as the solicitor downstairs pays him a visit just before he does a bunk. And I find a visitor pass in his pocket. Sounds like he's up to his neck in it.'

'I reckon, boss.'

'Anything else? What about James Kasper?'

'Nothing much. That passport seems kosher. Belongs to an online journalist. He looks into conspiracy theory stuff. I checked and he hasn't posted for a few days. Last post he said he was looking into something big. No details.'

'That sounds like something. Keep digging on him.'

'Hang on!' He heard Chambers' muffled voice call out in the background.

Harding was talking to her for a bit before he came back on the line. 'Guess what, your Alma Wilson, is big star of OnlyFans, and has made a lot of money by the sounds.'

'We know. Anything else?'

'There's more. She's almost married three convicted murderers. But they all fell through for whatever reason. Looks like she has a type.'

'Is one of them Keel?'

'Looks like she's been in communication with him. Maybe he was to be her fourth?'

Moone sighed, feeling himself sinking deeper into the mud. 'So, we've got two possible connections. Oh, by the way, Keith, can you look up...'

The line went empty. No sound. He stared at Butler. 'The line's gone dead.'

'No, boss, I'm still here. Think I pressed something by accident. Sorry.'

Moone let out a ragged breath. 'Don't give me a

heart attack, Harding. Anyway, check out a DS Ben Thurston. Short dark, greying hair. Stocky. He's just turned up here and we don't know who to trust. Keep digging.'

'Oh, we will. I'll call when we've got something.'

The call ended so Moone turned to Butler who was leaning against the door frame, arms folded. 'So, John and Alma are in the frame.'

She huffed. 'In the frame, but for what? We've got no bodies.'

He sighed, nodding as he moved closer. 'I know. But I know what I saw. George and his dog and Warren are missing. Where are they? Anyway, I thought you believed me.'

'I do. At least I believe you thought you saw two dead bodies. But what if you didn't?'

He frowned. 'What do you mean? You think I'm seeing things?'

'No, wally. What if someone's making it seem like they've been killed. I mean, take this Warren, or James Kasper? What was he up to?'

'Apparently, he's some online investigative journalist. Conspiracy theory stuff.'

She huffed. 'There you go. Maybe he's made it look like he's disappeared for some story or something…'

'What about George?'

'Maybe he's in on it. We don't know these people, we don't know their motives. This could be one big wind-up.'

Moone chewed it over. 'But it could be what it

looks like. Remember, one thing we know for sure is that we have an escaped murderer out there.'

'Yeah, probably looking like a prisoner flavoured ice lolly by now. Come on, let's go and ask some questions, if it'll make you feel better.'

Moone nodded and followed her back down to the bar. Everyone looked round at them as they entered, their eyes seemingly furtive. To Moone it felt like they all had something to hide.

'Anything?' Thurston said, back at the table and sipping his tea.

'Not much.' Moone turned to John. 'What were you doing at Channings Wood Prison?'

John blinked, staring at him, his face unreadable for a moment before he frowned. 'What are you talking about?'

'A solicitor visited Keel just before his escape. He had the same initials as you.'

John gave an empty laugh as he sat back. 'So? That's called a coincidence. I'm sure Keel has lots of visits from solicitors.'

Moone pulled up a chair and faced John. 'Thanks for lending me your coat earlier.'

'You're welcome.' John shrugged, smiling.

'I found a visitor badge in one of your pockets. From Channings Wood.'

John sat forward, looking surprised, his eyes darting round the room for a moment. 'What? No, no you didn't.'

'Yes, I did. Have a look yourself.'

John's eyes jumped to his coat. He reached for

it, then looked in the pockets. His eyebrows jumped as he took out the visitor badge. Moone thought he saw the flicker of anger reach his eyes before calm seemed to return. He held the badge between two fingers, as if he feared it might contaminate him in some way. 'I've never seen this before.'

'A likely story,' Butler said. 'Where did it come from, then?'

John stared at her. 'Someone planted it there.'

'Who?' Moone asked. 'Who would do that?'

'Someone who's been to Channings Wood Prison and doesn't want to admit it.' John put the badge on the table and then sat back, arms folded. 'It wasn't me.'

Moone looked at Alma and saw she was smirking, eyes fixed towards John. 'What about you, Alma?'

She straightened up, blinking, staring at Moone. She pointed a thumb at herself. 'Me? What have I done?'

'Apparently you have a type,' Butler said. 'You like them locked up.'

For a moment Alma was blank-faced, her eyes jumping between Moone and Butler. Then she shrugged it off. 'So? I like my men behind bars. So what?'

'Have you written to Keel?' Moone asked.

'Yes, murderers fascinate me,' she said and smiled. 'Is that a crime?'

'No,' Butler huffed. 'But I feel like it should be.'

Thurston stood up. 'So, you two have both

visited Channings Wood recently?'

'Not guilty,' John snapped. 'Someone planted that. You're the one who's been to that prison recently. Not me, mate.'

'I'm a police officer.'

'So you say. But you've got no ID.'

'He's not wrong.' Butler turned to Maggie. 'Can I have a coffee, please?'

Maggie smiled. 'Of course, love. Coming up.'

'Believe what you want,' Thurston said with heavy sigh. 'But I am a police officer and…'

There came a loud knock on the door. Everyone turned towards the sound, all falling silent as the wind continued to howl and whistle. The knock came again. John stood up, reaching for the bar stool again.

Butler held up her palm to him, then took out her Casco. 'You won't need that.'

'Who the hell is this now?' Tom asked, turning to face the door.

'Hello?!' a woman's voice called. 'Can we come in?'

'We?' John said, looking at Moone. 'Who the hell is we?'

'Let's find out,' Moone said and stepped towards the door and unlocked it. The door rattled, the wind hissing and grasping hold of it, ready to wrench it off its hinges. Moone opened it and guarded his eyes from the storm that bit at his face.

'Thank heavens,' a slender, brightly dressed woman said and slipped past Moone and entered the pub. She took off her bright red, fur-lined coat and yellow scarf. Moone was about to close the door, when a man barged past him and headed straight for the fire. He was average build, brown hair, a face that looked as if it had been carved out of marble and covered in stubble. He rubbed his hands, warming them on the flames.

'And who are you when you're at home?' Butler asked.

The woman, who looked to be in her forties, with long, greying brown hair, smiled at Butler and then put out her hand. 'Leslie. Leslie Pembroke. Thank goodness you were open. We've walked a long way.'

'Where have you come from?' Thurston said, walking up to the young man at the fire. But he didn't say anything.

'From Exeter,' Leslie said, straightening her clothes, then rubbing her hands together.

'Are you her son?' Thurston asked, stepping closer to the young man. To Moone it seemed as if the so-called copper was getting some kind of scent of trouble from the newcomer.

'Oh, no,' Leslie said with a laugh. 'I picked him up on the way. He was hitchhiking, weren't you, Eddie?'

'You picked up a hitchhiker?' John said, his eyes widening. 'In this day and age? Are you insane?'

The woman tilted her head as she smiled at him. 'If we can't help our stranded fellow humans, what are we?'

'Eddie what?' Thurston said, staring daggers at the young man. Eddie looked up from the fire sheepishly and said, in a quiet voice, 'Eddie Munslow.'

'Eddie Munslow.' Thurston nodded and stepped away, his attention seeming to turn to the woman. 'Where did you pick him up?'

'A couple of miles away from here. Why?'

Thurston stepped up close to her. 'Are you aware there's an escaped murderer on the loose?'

She laughed. 'Eddie wouldn't hurt a fly, would you, Eddie?'

'You hardly know him,' John said.

'Would you hurt a fly?' Alma said and moved close to the young lad. She put a hand on his arm. He stared at it, then looked up at her. 'No, I wouldn't.'

Alma huffed, then abruptly turned away. 'Why is everyone so boring round here?'

'You want excitement, miss?' Thurston snapped. 'Go out there. There's a man waiting to put his hands around your throat and squeeze the life out of you.'

Alma sat down at her table, sipped her drink and smiled at him. 'Sounds like my type.'

Leslie laughed awkwardly, then smiled at Maggie. 'Could we get a tea and... what will you have, Eddie? Tea, coffee or something stronger?'

'Tea... please,' he said, almost to himself.

'Do you pick up strangers often?' Butler asked her, standing beside her at the bar.

'I tend to help people in need. Don't you believe

in helping people?'

'I'm a police officer, so yes, but I don't think women should pick up hitchhikers. You're asking for trouble.'

'You're a police officer?' Leslie smiled even brighter. 'Then you should understand. Especially being a woman in that institution.'

'Here we go, the old bleeding heart,' John said, and laughed.

Leslie glared at him. 'Better a bleeding heart than having one made of stone.'

John laughed again, shaking his head. 'I look forward to reading about you in the papers when some scumbag cuts your liberal throat.'

'OK, that's enough,' Moone said. 'We're trapped here until this storm stops and the roads are clear. Let's try not to get on each other's nerves.'

'What about your two missing people?' Thurston asked, putting his empty mug on the bar.

'There's not much to be done. We'll have to wait it out.'

'Wait?' Alma said. 'Wait for someone else to disappear, you mean?'

Moone looked at her. 'No. That's not what I mean. If we all stick together, right here in this pub, then we'll be fine.'

'Will we?' Hannah said, looking down at the table. Then she looked up at Moone, a strained expression on her face. 'What if they're here? In this pub?'

The room grew quiet again, the wind filling the

void.

'Let's just stick together,' Butler said. 'We'll be fine.'

'I'm sorry,' Leslie said, turning round to face them all, looking confused. 'What are you talking about? Who's in this pub? And who's disappeared?'

'Two people so far,' Thurston said. 'From this pub.'

'Are you having some kind of murder mystery evening?' she asked, a nervous smile forming.

'No, you silly woman,' John said. 'Two people have disappeared. Real people. If you're not careful, you'll be next.'

'That's enough!' Thurston snapped and pointed at him.

'Is that how he does it?' Butler said.

Moone looked at her and saw she was staring intently at Thurston.

'Who does what?' the so-called copper said.

'You said he strangles the life out of them. Is that what Keel does?'

Thurston stared at her, still for a while before he nodded. 'Yeah. That's what he does. He starts, he stops. He looks them in the eyes. He likes to watch the life drain out of them. I think he thinks he's absorbing some of their… spirit, whatever you want to call it.'

'Well, sounds like another stupid criminal,' John said, getting comfortable. 'I mean, he got caught, didn't he?'

Thurston walked closer to him. 'I wouldn't call

him stupid. Don't underestimate Keel. I bet he's smarter than you.'

'Where's the barmaid gone?' Leslie said, leaning over the bar. 'She's taking a long time with the teas.'

Moone turned and stared at Butler. Then they both went hurrying around the bar and along the corridor, calling her name. There came no reply. Moone hurried along and found a doorway to a large, untidy kitchen. There was a long table at the centre and a massive Aga style oven. A kettle was whistling on the hob, but there was no Maggie.

'Where the hell has she gone?' Butler said, standing in the doorway, her eyes jumping round the kitchen.

Moone's gut went into spin cycle. But he refused to accept what his instinct was telling him. 'Better check upstairs.'

Butler turned and hurried back out into the hallway, her boots hammering along the wood floor and up the stairs. Moone took the kettle off the hob then followed her as she headed up the stairs and onto the landing.

'Maggie?' she called. 'Maggie? Where are you?'

Moone stopped dead when he thought he heard a sound. When Butler looked ready to call out again, he raised a finger to his lips. There it was again, a muffled cry and it seemed to be coming from the back bedroom. Butler pointed the way, then pulled out her Casco baton, whipped it to full length and headed towards the back of the house. Moone went after her as he pulled out the pepper spray.

The back room was like all the other bedrooms, plain, barely decorated and functional. A made-up double bed sat at the centre of the large room, with a large, Victorian style wardrobe opposite. As Moone listened, he heard the muffled cry again. The wardrobe. He pointed to it, so Butler put one hand on the handle, the other raising her Casco baton.

Moone nodded.

Butler yanked open the door. At the bottom, half covered by men's clothing, was Maggie, her eyes filled with relief, while a belt had been tied round her head and some cloth stuffed in her mouth. Butler lifted her out and undid her gag.

'Oh my God, thank you,' Maggie said as they helped her to her feet. 'I've never been so scared.'

'What happened?' Moone asked.

'I don't know. I went to the kitchen, and I'd just put the kettle on the stove when I was grabbed from behind. Whoever it was put a hand over my mouth and pulled me up the stairs.'

'Did you get a look at them?' Butler asked, as she undid another belt that had been strapped around Maggie's wrists.

'No, he was behind me, but they were wearing a dark coat or cloak or something. He shoved me headfirst into the cupboard, tied my hands and shut the door.'

Moone was about to say something when someone started shouting for them downstairs. Butler exchanged a look of exhaustion with him, before he left her and Maggie and hurried back down to the bar to see what was going on.

When he found everyone, or almost everyone, they were stood staring at the open door, the snow and the wind clawing at them. He looked around, counting bodies and saw that Thurston and Tom were missing.

'What happened?' he snapped.

Most of them blinked out of their frozen state and stared at him. Hannah lifted a finger and pointed at the doorway.

'They went out there,' she said, her voice strained. 'Tom went out there!'

Moone hurried to the door and tried to see something, any sign of them beyond the whirlwind of snow and darkness. The cold bit at his skin as he tried to make sense of anything in the snowy wasteland. He looked at Hannah. 'Why did they go out?'

'I saw the man again,' Alma said quietly. She had her eyes down on her drink.

'What man?' Moone asked.

She looked up, no signs of her usual smirk. 'The hooded figure. The one I saw before.'

'You've had too many gin and tonics,' John laughed. 'You're seeing things, darling.'

Alma gave him the middle finger before looking at Moone. 'Thurston went racing out there to see… he ordered Tom to go with him. Bloody idiot.'

Moone faced the wind and snow again, blinking into the darkness. A shape cut through the whiteness, a shroud coming fast towards him. He pulled out the pepper spray, pointing it towards the figure.

Thurston burst towards him, his hood up, his face red and covered in flakes of snow. He was breathing hard, doubled over as he pushed Moone aside. 'Close the door.'

'Where's Tom?!' Hannah rushed towards the door but Thurston grabbed her round the waist.

'I sent him back!' Thurston grunted as he wrestled with her, pulling her back from the door. 'Calm down!'

When he let go of Hannah and she retreated back a few steps, her whole body trembling, Moone grabbed Thurston by the arm.

'Where is he?' Moone growled.

'I sent him back here, I already said!' Thurston yanked his arm away. 'I only went out there when she said she saw someone out there.'

Alma snorted and rolled her eyes. 'Who's she? The cat's mother?'

'Well, we can't leave him out there!' Moone grabbed the door and pushed it against the angry wind.

'I'll come with you!' Thurston followed him.

Moone forced the door open, the wind immediately ripping at it. Snow blasted straight into his face, stinging his skin and sucking out the breath from his lungs. The storm had grown worse; a white void determined to swallow every shape and sound.

Thurston pulled his hood over his head and leaned into the gale. 'We won't last long out here,' he shouted over the roar.

'We don't have a choice,' Moone snapped back. 'Tom's out there somewhere!'

They both forced the door shut behind them. The noise of the storm swallowed the pub instantly and they could barely hear each other, let alone anything else. The world had become nothing but a white chaos and biting cold.

Moone hunched his shoulders, holding the pepper spray tight in his right hand.

'Tom!' he shouted into the void.

Thurston cupped his hands around his mouth. 'Tom!'

Nothing. Only the storm answered with a low, endless howl.

They trudged forward, their shoes crunching deep into the snow with every step. Moone looked down at the white ground to see if he could make out any footprints, but the constant snow had already covered them in another white blanket. His eyes streamed from the wind, each blink freezing his lashes together.

'We should turn back!' Thurston bellowed. 'It's pointless. He's not out here!'

'He is!' Moone shouted, though doubt gnawed at him already. He pushed on, half-blind, heart hammering. He scanned the swirling snow, searching for any sign of movement, a shadow, a silhouette. Anything at all.

Then something shifted.

Far ahead, maybe a hundred, maybe two

hundred yards, a figure was standing in the middle of the blizzard. A hooded shape. Whoever they were, they were standing completely still, watching Moone, staring deep into him.

Moone froze where he stood. His breath caught in his throat as his pulse thumped in his ears. The snow distorted everything, shadows twisted and stretched, but the figure was there. It was a man-shaped darkness in a chaotic world of white. The figure didn't move.

'Thurston...' Moone said. But the man hadn't heard.

Moone tapped his back, then pointed towards the shape.

It was gone.

Thurston grabbed Moone's arm. 'There's nothing there! Let's go back!'

Moone blinked the snowflakes from his lashes, squinting hard into the storm.

The figure was definitely gone.

Just like that, as if the snow had swallowed him whole.

'I saw him,' Moone muttered, more to himself than Thurston. 'There was someone there.'

'Your eyes are playing tricks,' Thurston said, gripping Moone's coat sleeve. 'Tom isn't out here. If he was, we'd have heard him screaming by now. We need to turn back.'

Moone swallowed hard, then nodded. His face burned with cold. His legs trembled from pushing through the snow. It felt as if the storm was alive, and intent on battling against them. It seemed to be winning. He forced himself to turn towards the lights of the pub. Through the white chaos, faint and blurred, the amber glow of the Scurry Inn flickered like a dying ember.

'Come on!' Thurston urged. 'Move before we get lost!'

Moone nodded. They fought their way back, each step a battle. The wind shoved them sideways, the snow clawing at their eyes, trying to blind them. Twice Moone stumbled. Thurston dragged him upright by the coat. They pushed on, breaths sharp and painful.

When they finally stumbled back through the pub door, the warmth hit them like a wall. They slammed the door shut behind them, both collapsing against it, both of them panting.

Inside, the pub had erupted into chaos.

Hannah stood near the centre of the room, pale, almost transparent, hands shaking uncontrollably. Her breath was coming in sharp, broken gasps as tears streamed down her cheeks.

Butler was standing by her.

'Where is he?! Where is Tom?!' Hannah cried, voice cracking. 'You said he'd come back! You said…'

Moone opened his mouth, half-frozen. 'We didn't see him… I'm sorry…'

But Hannah wasn't listening. Her knees had buckled as she clutched at the table beside her. Butler reached out a hand but was too late.

Hannah collapsed, her eyes rolling back as she

fainted.

The room fell dead silent except for the wind clawing at the windows and the frantic hammering of Moone's own heart.

SEVEN

Someone had suggested putting Hannah in one of the bedrooms, but Moone pointed out it was too dangerous. They needed to stick together, that was what was important now, so they made a bed out of the bench seat which was behind John's armchair. She now lay there, covered by a blanket, a pillow under her head, asleep.

Moone stared at her for a moment, but he couldn't see Hannah, just Alice. He gave himself a shake and looked around the room, taking stock. He noticed Leslie and Eddie weren't there.

'Where are they?' he asked, looking over the others.

'Who?' Butler asked.

'Leslie and Eddie.'

'Oh, Liberal Leslie and psycho Eddie,' John said, shaking his head. 'Eddie went to fetch some wood. She's in the toilet.'

Moone looked at Butler, then nodded towards the ladies' toilet. She sighed and walked to the toilet door and knocked.

'Leslie?' she called, then pushed the door open.

'Leslie! Are you in there?'

Butler stood back as Leslie came out, straightening her clothes and smiling. She stopped dead when she saw everyone was staring at her.

'What's happened?' she asked, her eyes widening.

'Another one bites the dust,' John said, smirking.

'The snow,' Alma said, then sipped her drink. 'Another one bites the snow.'

John nodded as if he approved.

'What is it with you two?' Butler asked, arms folded.

John sat back, eyebrows raised. 'I'm sorry, officer, what do you mean?'

Butler looked between them. 'It's obvious you two know each other. What's the story?'

'I've never met this man before,' Alma said.

Butler huffed. 'Are you a vegetarian, Alma?'

Alma narrowed her eyes. 'Yes, why?'

'When John fetched a sausage roll for you, he handed you a veggie one. Automatically picked a veggie one, not a meat one, and handed it to you.'

'Lucky guess,' John said.

Butler shook her head. 'No, luck had nothing to do with it. Come on, what's the story?'

Alma sat upright and glared at John. 'Idiot.'

'Shut up,' he said, his voice rigid. Then he let out a breath and nodded. 'All right. If you must know I'm a journalist. I've been to the prison a few times to try and talk to Keel. No dice, so then I ran into Alma here and I learned about her obsession with murderers…'

'Love affair, I prefer to call it,' Alma said, smiling to herself.

'Whatever,' John said. 'I persuaded her to write to Keel and try and get to see him so she could do some digging. We've spent a lot of time together, that's how I know she's a vegetarian. And yes, I pretended to be a solicitor so I could talk to him, but it didn't work. OK?'

Butler looked at Moone, so he shrugged. He'd been watching John carefully and saw nothing there that said he was lying. But then he wasn't sure his senses were up to much; he recalled seeing the eerie hooded shape outside, in the middle of the blizzard. But not for the first time. He remembered seeing the same shape near the hanging post, and part of him was almost willing to believe the village was haunted by a vengeful spirit. The sensible part told him to get a bloody grip.

'Well, I'm keeping an eye on you both.' Butler pointed a finger at John then Alma, who just raised her glass as if to say cheers.

When she stepped back and got shoulder to shoulder with Moone, Butler whispered, 'What the hell do you make of all this?'

'I don't know. But we've got three missing people.'

'And a dog.'

He nodded. 'Yep. We need to stay together. Keep an eye on each other.'

'We said that before and now look at us,

another one down. What do we do about Tom?'

'I really don't know. But we can't risk going out there again. I'm hoping the blizzard will let up.'

'I'm hoping this sort of thing doesn't happen every Christmas.'

He laughed, then looked round when he heard a door opening. Maggie was pulling open a door and letting Eddie through. In his arms was a pile of logs that he carried over to the dying fire. He knelt down and started throwing them on.

Thurston stood by him, arms folded, his expression like stone. 'Where were you all this time?'

'Getting the firewood,' Eddie said quietly. He stood up and wiped his hands on his jeans, his eyes fixed on the flames that had now grown hungry again.

'Convenient.'

Eddie shrugged but kept quiet as he turned and sat at the table. Maggie had gone through the door again and returned carrying a tray with a bowl of soup on it.

'Here you go, Eddie,' she said and put the soup and a spoon in front of him. 'It's only out of a tin, so don't get too excited.'

'Thanks.' Eddie picked up the spoon in one hand and rested his free arm around the bowl as if he feared someone might snatch it away. As Moone watched him eat, he noticed Thurston was watching him too, but even more intently. The so-called copper seemed to have a bee in his bonnet over the lad.

'Moone,' Thurston said, then nodded towards the bar. 'A word.'

Moone exchanged a look with Butler, then joined the man at the bar, their backs to the room.

'Did you see it?' Thurston whispered.

'What am I supposed to have seen?'

'The way Eddie's eating.'

Moone looked over his shoulder. 'With a spoon?'

Thurston sighed. 'Some detective you are. That's the way they eat in prison. One handed, while the other hand guards your food and yourself. Eddie's been inside.'

'You think Eddie's Keel?'

'No, too young. But what if he knows Keel? What if he's here to meet him or help him?'

Moone looked over at the lad again. It was possible, of course. Perhaps he was right, Moone thought as he watched the guarded way Eddie was eating. 'You'd better keep an eye on him, then.'

Thurston narrowed his eyes. 'So, you believe I'm on the job too?'

Moone shrugged. 'I suppose. What do you think's going on here?'

'I'm not sure. But if Keel is doing this, why is he making everyone disappear? His victims were single women, usually in their forties. He'd rob them blind, then strangle them. This doesn't fit, does it?'

Moone shook his head. 'Not really. But what if he was trying to make his way here and you're right and one of these lot was here to pick him up?'

Thurston nodded. 'Sounds more plausible, doesn't it? But again, why make everyone disappear?'

Moone was running it all through his frozen brain and coming up empty, apart from a niggling feeling that had started to scratch at him, a sense that something or someone was out of place. Whatever it was, it escaped him. 'I don't know, but I've got this feeling I'm missing something. Something is staring me in the face, but I just can't see it.'

'It'll come.' Thurston patted his arm then asked Maggie for another tea.

'Did someone say there's a lad lost outside?' Leslie said.

Moone turned and faced her, the guilt crawling up his spine and sitting heavy on his shoulders. 'Tom. We've been out to look for him, but we couldn't find him.'

'Well, I'll go looking for him!' Leslie made a grab for her coat.

'Nobody's going out there!' Butler snapped. 'You'll just get lost. We need to stay together.'

Leslie stared at her, looking horrified. 'You're just going to let him freeze to death? What sort of person are you? What sort of people are any of you? He's out there freezing to death and...'

'Shut up, you silly woman!' John groaned. 'Anyone else who goes out there will just end up the same way. They tried to find him, they couldn't. End of story.'

'Sit down, love,' Alma said. 'Have a gin and tonic, it'll set you free.'

Leslie looked around at everyone accusingly as she put her coat back. 'I don't drink.'

'See, there's your first problem,' Alma said and laughed.

Moone turned to Butler and lowered his voice. 'She's right though. I should go out there and have another look.'

'But what if you disappear? What am I supposed to do?'

He smiled. 'Mourn for a couple of years, then eventually stop wearing black, I suppose.'

'Funny. If you do go, don't go alone.'

Moone nodded, then looked over the room. 'But who can I trust? The obvious choice is Thurston, but how do we know he's really a copper?'

'We don't. Take the Casco and the pepper spray. First sign of trouble, spray him and whack him.'

Moone shook his head, then headed over to Thurston. 'I'm going to have another look for Tom.'

Thurston nodded. 'Good. I'll come with you. Let me get my coat on.'

Moone put his coat back on, then turned to the room. 'We're going to look for Tom again. Everyone stay here. No one goes anywhere.'

There were only a few moans and a little chatter from the rest of them, so he turned and headed out into the blizzard again as Thurston pushed the door open.

The cold hit Moone like a wall of ice. He stooped instinctively, pulling his coat tight around him as the blizzard clawed at his face. Snowflakes stung like grit. Thurston shoved the door shut behind them, muffling the chorus of voices inside the Scurry Inn, and for a moment they both stood there, half-blind, half-deaf, swallowed by the whiteness again.

'Christ almighty,' Thurston muttered, squinting into the gale. 'This is pointless!'

Moone didn't answer, just forced himself forward, his shoes sinking into the snow like it was icy quicksand. Somewhere in the distance the shapes of the village houses crowded in together for warmth. He cupped his hands around his mouth and shouted, 'TOM!'

His voice was whipped away instantly, swallowed whole by the wind.

Thurston trudged up beside him, one glove grasping his hood to stop it ripping back. 'I'm telling you now, the lad's not out here. If he is, then he's a goner. No one could last long in this.'

Moone ignored him and pushed on, thinking of Hannah, the wreck of a girl. They skirted past the pub's signpost, its metal chains screeching as it swung wildly above them. The snowdrifts deepened as they went, covering their boots, and eventually their shins.

'Tom!' Moone shouted again. 'TOM!'

Nothing. No voice returned to them, only the roar of the storm and the distant slam of something hitting the side of a building.

They made it as far as the narrow lane that seemed to lead towards the village centre. The outline of the old stone church loomed ahead, the bell tower just a darker smear against the sky. Moone blinked snow from his lashes.

Something moved.

A flicker.

A shape.

There it was again. A hooded figure was standing at the mouth of the alley that ran beside the church.

'There!' Moone grabbed Thurston's arm. 'Did you see that?'

'See what?! There's nothing there!' Thurston yelled.

Moone didn't bother to wait and stumbled forward, forcing his legs to move through the heavy snow. When he reached the alley, he swung the beam of the phone's torch across the narrow gap between the church wall and the house opposite.

Nothing. No shape, only darkness and swirling white.

For a moment he stood there, chest heaving, heart thudding. The wind howled between the buildings, a low, eerie whistle that tugged at his clothes and made him shiver.

'Moone?' Thurston called behind him. 'We need to get back. Now!'

Moone nodded and started to turn away...

He stopped, his body trembling all over as his eyes jumped to something in the snow.

A trainer.

A white trainer sticking out from a pile of snow against the wall.

His stomach lurched.

Tom? Sickness rose as far as his chest but he forced it down as he reached out his burning, cold hands.

'Help me dig!' he barked, already dropping to his knees.

Thurston swore and crouched beside him, scraping at the snow with frantic, gloved hands. The cold burned Moone's skin as he cleared the drift, pushing snow aside until he uncovered a leg, then jogging bottoms... then a grey sweatshirt stretched tight across a frozen chest. The face appeared last, brown hair crusted with ice, the beard stiff with frost, the eyes closed.

Thurston flinched. 'That's prison kit.'

Moone stared at the dead man, his own breath pluming fast into the air. He felt the world tilt for a moment as he processed it.

'Is it Keel?' he whispered.

Thurston leaned in, scanning the features, then nodded once, sharply. 'That's him. That's definitely him. Keel's dead. Looks like the cold got him.'

Moone leaned over the frozen body, examining his hair and head that was encrusted with snow. His eyes jumped to the pink and red snow clinging to the back of his skull. He looked around at Thurston. 'Well, he didn't die of hypothermia. Someone's smashed his skull in.'

Thurston took a look, then nodded. 'You're right. Couldn't have happened to a nicer individual.'

Moone sat back on his heels, his heart still pounding. There was a mix of emotions fighting for supremacy in his chest. Relief. Confusion. Then came the new, terrible understanding that was beginning to take shape in his frozen brain.

If Keel was dead...

Then whoever was taking people...

'Moone.'

Thurston was now stood up and staring behind them. Moone turned his head. Across the white ground, back towards the Scurry Inn, one of the upstairs windows was lit with an unnatural, harsh white beam that spilled through the gaps in the curtains. The light was moving.

Then a silhouette moved across the window.

Slow.

Deliberate.

Then it was gone.

'Someone's upstairs,' Thurston said. 'Who the hell is that?'

Moone got to his feet. 'We need to get back. Now.'

They both hurried over the snow, through the wind, hunched over, covered head to foot in white, looking like two ghosts lost in limbo. The storm battered them from all sides, pushing them off course, clawing at their eyes. Moone blinked hard, vision blurring, and for a moment he thought he saw another figure moving in front of the pub.

Tom?

But when he looked again, there was nothing.

EIGHT

The lights of the pub flickered through the haze, a dim orange glow that seemed impossibly far away. Moone forced himself onwards, his boots slipping, breath burning in his lungs.

'Moone!' Thurston shouted over the wind. 'Hurry up!'

They reached the door, half-frozen, shivering, the panic racing through them. Moone grabbed the handle with his numb fingers. He took one last look over his shoulder at the church, the alley, and the empty white world before he pushed the door open and they stumbled back into the light.

Everyone stared at them as they shook the snow off.

'Who's upstairs?' Thurston demanded, his eyes jumping round the room. 'Who is it?'

Butler stared at him. 'No one's upstairs. We're all here.'

'Someone's up there!' he grunted, then headed round the bar and through the door. Moone followed fast behind and they both raced up the wooden stairs, the only sound being the blood thumping in his ears and the thud of their boots on the steps.

The landing was in darkness. None of the rooms were lit up. Thurston slowed down and edged his way towards the room they had been looking up at. But it was in darkness like all the other bedrooms. Moone took out the Casco and flicked it to full length. He went into the room slowly, sliding his hand up the wall. He found the light switch and turned on the light.

There was a bed, an old sofa, a wardrobe. He checked under the bed while Thurston looked into the empty wardrobe.

'Well, no one's here,' Thurston said, taking another look round the room. 'You saw them too, didn't you?'

Moone nodded, then faced the stairs. 'They had time to get back downstairs.' Moone was running it all through his brain again, then stared out the window. 'When we were out there, they were in here. Why?'

Thurston shrugged. 'Looking for something?'

Moone nodded. 'Looking for something. And why was Keel here? Was he looking for something? Maybe he knew this place and he'd stashed something here or he was meeting someone here. Warren, or Kasper, was the only one staying here. What if he was here to meet Keel?'

Thurston raised his eyebrows. 'You're pretty smart, Moone.'

'Thanks. I have my moments. Let's search Kasper's stuff again.'

Moone found Warren's room. The suitcase was still open on the bed, the clothes neat and folded. He went over and started pulling the clothes out and searching every item. Nothing.

Then he looked into the suitcase. He put his hands on the bottom and felt along it. His fingers touched something, a rectangle the size of a passport. He grasped hold of the material and tore it away.

'Bloody hell,' Thurston said, looking over Moone's shoulder. There was a British passport taped to the bottom of the case. Moone pulled it away, opened it up and saw a photograph of a man with a hard face and dead eyes. The passport was in the name of David O'Neil. He showed it to Thurston, who nodded and said, 'That's Keel. So, Warren was here to meet him and then they were taking off somewhere.'

'With whatever they were after. I'm thinking money.'

'So Keel was sneaking in the pub to look for his ill-gotten gains. Crafty bastard.'

Moone had his doubts as he looked towards the window and wild snow that still tore across the darkness.

'Keel's been dead for hours, I reckon, although I'm no expert. I don't think it was him sneaking in.'

Thurston scratched his stubble. 'Then who?'

Moone didn't reply. A theory had started to grow in his mind but he wanted confirmation. He went to the phone and dialled the station. Harding answered after a couple of rings.

'How's it going, boss?' Harding asked.

'Keel's dead,' he said. 'We found him frozen in the snow but someone had already caved his head in.'

'Jesus. So you've still got a killer on the loose?'

Moone nodded, sensing Thurston standing behind him in the doorway. 'Looks like it. What did you find out about Keel? Did he pull any big jobs before he was caught?'

'Er... yeah, as it happens, he did. They hit a cash handling depot near Bristol. Not all the money was recovered. Then Keel was caught after he strangled those women, but he never said where the money was.'

'I think it's here, in this pub.'

'Really? They reckon it's nearly half a million.'

Moone nodded, running his theory through his head, not quite convinced it held water. 'Did Keel work with or have a connection with anyone called George?'

'Hang on. I'm looking at his extensive history. Well, all I can see is his old man. Ernie George Keel. He was a right ruthless bastard in his day, by the look.'

'How old would he be?'

'In his seventies.'

Moone ran a hand down his face. 'I think someone's been laughing at us this whole time.'

'Boss?'

'Never mind. How are the roads?'

'Still blocked. Oh, by the way, I checked up on that detective, Thurston?'

'And?' Moone could see the blurry shape of Thurston in the doorway.

'There was a detective called Thurston with Exeter Police, but he was kicked out for taking backhanders and other dodgy stuff...'

Moone slowly turned and saw Thurston standing rigid, his eyes fixed on him. In his right hand was a carving knife.

'Put the phone down, Moone,' he said, his voice more of a growl than anything.

Moone hung up. 'So, you with Keel or what?'

He gave an empty laugh. 'You're smart, Moone. Smarter than I thought. You can figure it out.'

Moone let out a shaky breath, wondering if he was going to get out of the room without a knife being stuck in him. 'You killed Keel?'

'That's a bit of a tongue twister, but yeah, I did. He was in a cell with this other lowlife scumbag called Barrett. Well, Barrett owed me a favour, sort of, so I got him to find out what Keel was planning. Turns out it was to come here and meet Terry Garnett, that's Warren, or Kasper, to you. Somehow he must have stolen the real James Kasper's identity. Garnett's just another thug, but he's got connections. Their plan, find the money and then head off to some shithole country with no extradition treaty. Same old story.'

'What about you? Apparently, you were kicked off the force for taking backhanders.'

'Bollocks. I was fitted up. All right, I took a couple of gifts from people I shouldn't have. Then I was fitted up in some sting operation. No pension. Debt up to my eyes. Well, that ends today.'

'You have to find the money first.'

Thurston grinned, then laughed. 'I found the money. Keel had it. He'd hidden it in the house across the way, buried it under the shed. He didn't even hear me coming, stupid bastard. I picked up a shovel... anyway, I don't feel bad for him, not after all those girls he killed.'

'So, what now?'

'We go back downstairs. Come on.' Thurston moved back, giving Moone enough room to slip out the doorway. He moved slowly, keeping an eye on the knife as he passed.

'Go on, downstairs, Moone. Time to join the rest of the party.'

As Moone reached the stairs, he said, 'So, do you know who's been sneaking in, looking for the loot?'

'Of course. Ernie George Keel. But I didn't care because I already had the money.'

'But you couldn't leave because of the roads.'

'That's right. I just had to ride it out. But it looks like the snow's stopping now.'

Moone looked across the landing and through to one of the bedroom windows. No longer did the snowflakes rush past, and soon the roads would clear. Moone carried on down the stairs, sensing Thurston behind him. He went back into the bar and saw everyone else sitting around. Maggie was behind the bar. She smiled at Moone, but shock widened her eyes as she spotted the knife in Thurston's hand.

'Where have you two been?' Butler asked, then her face changed too, losing the look of annoyance.

'Keel's dead,' Moone said, stepping around the bar. 'Thurston killed him.'

The bent copper stopped close to Maggie who was staring at the knife with horror-struck eyes.

'That's right,' Thurston said. 'And I've got the money. I've also got a fast car stashed around the corner, and now the snow's stopping, I'll be off soon. You lot just behave yourselves and no one has to get hurt.'

'So it was you all along?' Butler said with a huff.

'No, not me,' Thurston said, his watchful eyes jumping to everyone in the bar. 'That was probably Ernie Keel, the murderer and thief's old man. He must have found out about the money being here somehow and he's been looking for it.'

'Ernie Keel?' Butler looked at Moone.

'George. We thought he'd been murdered but it was faked, giving him time to search.' Moone had a thought. 'What about Tom? He went out with you.'

'Tied up in the house across the way. He's safe. I'm not a psycho like Keel was. Now, it remains to find Ernie.'

'He's not here,' Moone said.

Thurston shook his head. 'Oh, he's here all right. There's one place you haven't looked. The cellar. Pubs have cellars, Moone. It's in the storeroom. Maggie, be a love and tell him to come out before I make sure he never gets out.'

Maggie looked confused, but moved slowly through the door. Her footsteps trailed off. There was a creaking sound, then voices. Moone could hear a gruff voice.

Maggie came back in and Thurston told her to stand back where she was. A shadow fell into the room, then it was followed by the old man they knew as George. But the look of confusion and bewilderment he wore before had been replaced by a look of slow burning malice.

'Well, hello there, Ernie,' Thurston said. 'Join the party. John, Alma, tie him to a chair.'

Alma begrudgingly got up from her seat as she said, 'Just as I was beginning to enjoy myself watching the show.'

'What are we going to tie him up with?' John said, eyebrows raised.

Thurston reached into his pocket and brought out some cable ties and threw them over the bar. 'I'm always prepared, just like a boy scout. Strap his arms and legs to the chair. Hurry up.'

Alma and John went to work, strapping the old man down to the chair, while Ernie sat staring at Thurston, a dark glare on his face.

'I'll find you,' Ernie said through his teeth.

'No, you won't. I'm good at disappearing.' Thurston looked around the bar, smiling. 'Well, it's been fun, hasn't it? And cosy?'

'Yeah,' Alma agreed. 'It's like one of those

murder mystery parties.'

'Shut up,' Butler said, then stared at the bent copper with the knife. 'Go on then, sling your hook.'

'Oh, don't worry, I plan to.' Thurston moved towards Maggie, so she stepped back, out of his way. 'The money's in the boot of my car, ready for a quick getaway.'

Then Moone saw Maggie's eyes jump to the underside of the bar. While Thurston moved towards the end of it, Maggie reached under the bar and came out with a baseball bat. Before anyone could protest, she had swung it and cracked him hard on the head. His legs buckled, his knife hand falling. Moone and Butler took the chance and stormed forward, grabbed his arms and restrained him.

They had him cuffed and face down on the floor before he had the chance to fight back. Then they heaved him up and strapped him to another chair. His head lolled as he seemed to fall into unconsciousness.

Butler let out a heavy breath as she wiped her hands on her trousers. 'Well, looks like that's wrapped up.'

Moone nodded, although he still had a niggling feeling burrowing into the back of his brain. Whatever it was, it just wouldn't come. 'Yeah, looks like the snow's stopping too. Should be able to get backup here soon.'

It was Maggie who managed to dig out a radio and set it up on the bar. It crackled to life and they all sat there and listened to it in silence. Moone wanted to comment how nice it was that no one was on their phone, doom scrolling, and the fact that it was almost as if they had travelled back to a more civilised time. But then his eyes fell on the unconscious Thurston and the strangely quiet, but brooding Ernie Keel.

'I think the phone's ringing,' Maggie said.

Moone sighed, pulled himself up and then trudged back up the wooden stairs to the phone. 'Moone.'

'Hey boss,' Harding said. 'All OK? You hung up suddenly.'

'I did. Turns out Thurston was a wrong 'un and Ernie Keel was hiding in the cellar. Anyway, looks like it's all sorted.'

Moone was looking around the room, noticing the lack of decoration. None of the rooms seemed particularly looked after. None of them had the...

'Harding,' he said, his heart starting to beat a little faster. 'Ernie Keel. Did he have a wife, partner or associate?'

'Oh, yeah. Margaret Penfold. Why?'

'Moone!' Butler called out. 'Get down here!'

'Got to go. Send backup.' Moone hung up then went downstairs, pretty much knowing what he would find.

But he was still a little surprised when he saw

Alma and John cutting the straps off of Ernie Keel, while Maggie the landlady, or Margaret Penfold, was holding a knife to Hannah's throat.

'Join your mates,' Maggie said, her eyes jumping round the room. 'Hurry up before I slice her throat open. I will, I don't care.'

As Moone went around the bar and stood with the others who were backed up near the toilets, Keel stood up and stretched.

'Well done, sweetheart,' he said to Maggie as he grinned. He held out his hand to her. She put the knife in his palm. 'Let's go and find his car. Maggie, search his pockets.'

Maggie hurried over to the unconscious Thurston and started patting him down. Then she smiled as she pulled out a key fob and said, 'Bingo.'

'Open the door, you!' Keel barked as he snapped his fingers at Alma.

She rolled her eyes then took hold of the door and pushed it open. The wind had died down and the snow had stopped falling. A blanket of white covered the ground all the way to the dark silhouette of the village and the few lights that shone.

'Let's go, Maggie,' Keel said, moving towards the door, the large knife held out to everyone.

'What do we do?' Butler asked Moone under her breath.

'Let them go. They'll get picked up.'

They watched as the two figures lurched out of the door and trudged into the snow. After a minute or so, an engine rumbled to life. Then the sound got quieter.

Alma shut the door of the pub and shivered. 'Well, that was fun. Same time next Christmas?'

A little of the snow had started again and was being carried across the road. The headlights of the small car Maggie drove barely lit up the darkness. The car kept pulling to one side, the wheels slipping.

'We did it!' Keel said, then tapped the window with his fist and looked at Maggie. 'We bloody well did it. We'll be sipping margaritas in no time.'

'I thought I made a very good landlady.'

'I'll buy you a bar, sweetheart.'

Maggie laughed, then looked out into the road that now seemed so dark and filled with snow. 'I can hardly see a thing, Ernie. I thought the snow had stopped.'

'It's just a snowdrift,' he said. 'It'll pass in a minute. Keep going.'

'If you're sure.'

'I'm sure.'

The wind howled, buffeting the car, sweeping the drifting snow up in a swirl.

The cloaked shape appeared from nowhere. Standing directly in their path.

Maggie screamed and slammed on the brakes. The car spun and slid as she battled with the wheel. But to no avail. The car seemed to lift off, then they were turning, over and over.

Moone pulled his coat around him as the sun finally arrived, making a slow and orange appearance over the village. Now he could see the rest of Scurry-on-the-Moor, he realised how picturesque it really was. With the snow blanketing the ground, it looked every bit like a Christmas card. If it wasn't for the incident response cars and the ambulances, the scene would have been almost peaceful.

Butler came trudging through the snow, her breath clouding out of her mouth, her cheeks ruddy. But somehow she still looked beautiful.

'What are you staring at?' she said, narrowing her eyes at him. 'Take a photo, it'll last longer.'

He laughed, then nodded to the police cars. 'What's going on, then?'

'Tom's OK, so is the dog. They were both tied up in the house across the way. Warren, or should I say, Terry Garnett, is dead. Blunt-force trauma, same as Keel Junior.'

Moone saw one of the uniforms opening the back door of an incident response car. Then another two uniforms frogmarched Thurston towards it and guided him inside. Before the car took off, the bent copper turned and stared at them both with cold eyes.

'Merry Christmas to him too,' Butler said.

Moone nudged Butler when he saw Eddie leaving the pub arm in arm with Alma. 'I think...'

Butler glared at him. 'If you say something like you think this is the beginning of a beautiful friendship or something, I'll bloody clout you.'

He grinned, then stuffed his hands in his pockets. 'We'd better get back. It's Christmas Eve.'

She nodded. 'Come on then. Don't faff.'

'I knew you'd say that.'

As they climbed into the car, and Butler started it up, he caught sight of the rest of the guests leaving the Scurry Inn. There was Tom and Hannah hugging, both crying. With joy, he hoped as Butler drove them away.

'I've got a present for you, by the way,' Butler said.

He stared at her. 'Have you? What?'

She tutted. 'It's a surprise, you wally.'

'Gimme a clue.'

'No. You'll find out.'

'I've got you a present too.'

She smiled. 'I should hope so. You're lucky to have me, Moone.'

'Don't I know it.'

It was a little way ahead, along a lane that was still covered in a thick blanket of snow, that they saw the scorched, upturned car. There was a fire engine close by, parked near to an ambulance.

Butler slowed down and pulled in close to a uniformed officer who was guarding the scene.

'What happened?' she asked as she showed her ID.

'A couple skidded off the road, ma'am. Elderly

man and woman. She was driving. Both dead on impact. Found a load of money in the boot. Bit of a weird one.'

Butler drove them on, and after a moment's silence, she said, 'And then they were gone.'

GET TWO FREE AND EXCLUSIVE CRIME THRILLERS

I think building a relationship with the readers of my books is something very important, and makes the writing process even more fulfilling. Sign up to my mailing list and you'll receive two exclusive crime thrillers for FREE! Get SOMETHING DEAD- an Edmonton Police Station novella, and BITER- a standalone serial killer thriller.

Just visit markyarwood.co.uk

or you can find me here:

https://www.bookbub.com/authors/mark-yarwood

facebook.com/MarkYarwoodcrimewriter/

DID YOU ENJOY THIS BOOK?

YOU COULD MAKE A DIFFERENCE.

Because reviews are critical to the success of an author's career, if you have enjoyed reading this novel, please do me a massive favour by leaving one on Amazon.

Yes, I am happy to leave a review- Click here

_____

Reviews increase visibility. Your help in leaving one would make a massive difference to this author. Thank you for taking the time to read my work.

THE DCI
PETER MOONE
THRILLERS

BAD TIMES

TAKE YOUR LIFE

PREPARED TO DIE

OF RAGE AND RUIN

Get your FREE eBooks- visit
www.markyarwood.co.uk

'

THE EDMONTON POLICE STATION THRILLERS SERIES

THE EDMONTON POLICE STATION THRILLERS BOX SETS

THE EDMONTON POLICE STATION THRILLER SERIES: BOOKS 1-3

THE EDMONTON POLICE STATION THRILLER SERIES: BOOKS 4-6

THE DCI JAIRUS NOVELS

JAIRUS' SACRIFICE

JAIRUS' SLAUGHTER

JAIRUS' TORMENT

———————————

THE DCI JAIRUS NOVELS BOX SETS

THE DCI JAIRUS NOVELS: BOOKS 1-3

THE SEAN
FAINT SERIES

THE DCI PETER MOONE THRILLERS

BAD TIMES

TAKE YOUR LIFE

PREPARED TO DIE

Get your FREE eBooks- visit
www.markyarwood.co.uk

MARK YARWOOD

.

Printed in Dunstable, United Kingdom